T0114249

INTERNATIONAL

BOOKS BY *Vladimir Nabokov*

NOVELS
Mary
King, Queen, Knave
The Defense
The Eye
Glory
Laughter in the Dark
Despair
Invitation to a Beheading
The Gift
The Real Life of Sebastian Knight
Bend Sinister
Lolita
Pnin
Pale Fire
Ada or Ardor: A Family Chronicle
Transparent Things
Look at the Harlequins!

SHORT FICTION
Nabokov's Dozen
A Russian Beauty and Other Stories
Tyrants Destroyed and Other Stories
Details of a Sunset and Other Stories
The Enchanter

DRAMA
The Waltz Invention
Lolita: A Screenplay
The Man from the USSR and Other Plays

the eye

the eye

Vladimir Nabokov

VINTAGE INTERNATIONAL

VINTAGE BOOKS
A DIVISION OF RANDOM HOUSE, INC.
NEW YORK

Translated by Dmitri Nabokov
in collaboration with the author

FIRST VINTAGE INTERNATIONAL EDITION, SEPTEMBER 1990

Library of Congress Cataloging-in-Publication Data
Nabokov, Vladimir Vladimorovich, 1899–1977.
The eye / by Vladimir Nabokov—1st Vintage international ed.
p.   cm.—(Vintage international)
ISBN 0-679-72723-X
I. Title.
PS3527.A15E9 1990
813'.54—dc20   90-50265
CIP

To Véra

foreword

The Russian title of this little novel is SOGLYADATAY *(in traditional transliteration), pronounced phonetically "Sugly-dart-eye," with the accent on the penultimate. It is an ancient military term meaning "spy" or "watcher," neither of which extends as flexibly as the Russian word. After toying with "emissary" and "gladiator," I gave up trying to blend sound and sense, and contented myself with matching the "eye" at the end of the long stalk. Under that title the story weaved its pleasant way through three installments of* PLAYBOY *in the first months of 1965.*

I composed the original text in 1930, in Berlin—where my wife and I rented two rooms from a German family on quiet Luitpoldstrasse—and at the end of that year it appeared in the Russian emigré review "SOVREMENNYYA ZAPISKI" *in Paris. The people in the book are the favorite* characters of my literary youth: Russian expatriates living in Berlin, Paris, or London. Actually, of course, they might just as well have been Norwegians in Naples or Ambracians in Ambridge: I have always been indifferent to social problems, merely using the material that happened to be near, as a voluble diner pencils a street corner on the table cloth or arranges a crumb and two olives in a diagrammatic position between menu and salt cellar. One amusing result of this indifference to community life and to the intrusions of history is that the social group casually swept into artistic focus acquires a falsely permanent air; it is taken for granted at a certain time in a certain place, by the emigré writer and his emigré readers. The Ivan Ivanovich and Lev Osipovich of 1930 have long been replaced by non-Russian readers who are puzzled and irritated today by having to imagine a society they know nothing about; for I do not mind repeating again and again that bunches of pages have been torn out of the past by the destroyers of freedom ever since Soviet propaganda, almost half a century ago, misled foreign opinion into ignoring or denigrating the importance of Russian emigration (which still awaits its chronicler).

The time of the story is 1924-5. Civil War in Russia has ended some four years ago. Lenin has just died but his tyranny continues to flourish. Twenty German marks are not quite five dollars. The expatriates in the Berlin of the book range from paupers to successful businessmen. Examples of the latter are Kashmarin, Matilda's cauchemaresque husband (who evidently escaped from Russia by the southern route, via Constantinople), and the father of Evgenia and Vanya, an elderly gentleman (who judiciously directs the London branch of a German firm, and keeps a dancing girl). Kashmarin is probably what the English call "middleclass," but the two young ladies at 5 Peacock Street obviously belong to the Russian nobility, titled or untitled, which does not prevent them from having Philistine reading tastes. Evgenia's fat-faced husband, whose name sounds rather comic today, works in a Berlin bank. Colonel Mukhin, a nasty prig, fought in 1919 under Denikin, and in 1920 under Wrangel, speaks four languages, affects a cool, worldly air, and will probably do very well in the soft job into which his future father-in-law is steering him. Good Roman Bogdanovich is a Balt imbued with German, rather than Russian, culture. The eccentric Jew Weinstock, the pacifist woman doctor Marianna Nikolaevna, and the classless narrator himself are representatives of the many-faceted Russian intelligentsia. These tips should make things a little easier for the kind of reader who (like myself) is wary of novels that deal with spectral characters in unfamiliar surroundings, such as translations from the Magyar or the Chinese.

As is well known (to employ a famous Russian phrase), my books are not only blessed by a total lack of social significance, but are also mythproof: Freudians flutter around them avidly, approach with itching oviducts, stop, sniff, and recoil. A serious psychologist, on the other hand, may distinguish through my rain-sparkling crysto-grams a world of soul dissolution where poor Smurov only exists insofar as he is reflected in other brains, which in their turn are placed in the same strange, specular pre-dicament as his. The texture of the tale mimics that of detective fiction but actually the author disclaims all intention to trick, puzzle, fool, or otherwise deceive the reader. In fact, only that reader who catches on at once will derive genuine satisfaction from THE EYE. It is unlikely that even the most credulous peruser of this twinkling tale will take long to realize who Smurov is. I tried it on an old English lady, two graduate students, an ice-hockey coach, a doctor, and the twelve-year-old child of a neighbor. The child was the quickest, the neighbor, the slowest.

The theme of THE EYE is the pursuit of an investigation which leads the protagonist through a hell of mirrors and ends in the merging of twin images. I do not know if the keen pleasure I derived thirty-five years ago from adjust-ing in a certain mysterious pattern the various phases of the narrator's quest will be shared by modern readers, but in any case the stress is not on the mystery but on the pattern. Tracking down Smurov remains, I believe, excel-lent sport despite the passing of time and books, and the shift from the mirage of one language to the oasis of another. The plot will not be reducible in the reader's mind—if I read that mind correctly—to a dreadfully painful love story in which a writhing heart is not only spurned, but humiliated and punished. The forces of imagination which, in the long run, are the forces of good remain steadfastly on Smurov's side, and the very bitterness of tortured love proves to be as intoxicating and bracing as would be its most ecstatic requital.

Vladimir Nabokov

Montreux, April 19, 1965.

the eye

I MET THAT WOMAN, THAT MA-
tilda, during my first autumn of *émigré* existence in Berlin, in the early twenties of two
spans of time, this century and my foul life.
Someone had just found me a house tutor's job
in a Russian family that had not yet had time
to grow poor, and still subsisted on the phan-
tasmata of its old St. Petersburg habits. I had
had no previous experience in bringing up children—had not the least idea how to comport
myself and what to talk about with them.
There were two of them, both boys. In their
presence I felt a humiliating constraint.

They kept count of my smokes, and this
bland curiosity made me hold my cigarette at
an odd, awkward angle, as if I were smoking
for the first time; I kept spilling ashes in my

lap, and then their clear gaze would pass attentively from my hand to the pale-gray pollen gradually rubbed into the wool.

Matilda, a friend of their parents, often visited them and stayed on for dinner. One night, as she was leaving, and there was a noisy downpour, they lent her an umbrella, and she said: "How nice, thank you very much, the young man will see me home and bring it back." From that time on, walking her home was one of my duties. I suppose she rather appealed to me, this plump, uninhibited, cow-eyed lady with her large mouth, which would gather into a crimson pucker, a would-be rosebud, when she looked in her pocket mirror to powder her face. She had slender ankles and a graceful gait, which made up for many things. She exuded a generous warmth; as soon as she appeared, I would have the feeling that the heat in the room had been turned up, and when, after disposing of this large live furnace by seeing her home, I would be walking back alone amid the liquid sounds and quicksilver gloss of the pitiless night, I would feel cold, cold to the point of nausea.

Later her husband arrived from Paris and would come to dinner with her; he was a husband like any other, and I did not pay much

4

attention to him, except to notice the habit he had before speaking of clearing his throat into his fist with a rapid rumble; and the heavy bright-knobbed black cane with which he would tap on the floor while Matilda transformed the parting with her hostess into a buoyant soliloquy. After a month her husband left, and, the very first night I was seeing her home, Matilda invited me to come up to take a book she had been persuading me to read for a long time, something in French called *Ariane, Jeune Fille Russe*. It was raining as usual, and there were tremulous halos around the street lamps; my right hand was immersed in the hot fur of her moleskin coat; with my left I held an open umbrella, drummed upon by the night. This umbrella—later, in Matilda's apartment—lay expanded near a steam radiator, and kept dripping, dripping, shedding a tear every half-minute, and so managed to run up a large puddle. As for the book, I forgot to take it.

Matilda was not my first mistress. Before her, I was loved by a seamstress in St. Petersburg. She too was plump, and she too kept advising me to read a certain novelette (*Murochka, the Story of a Woman's Life*). Both of these ample ladies would emit, during the sex-

5

ual storm, a shrill, astonished, infantile peep, and sometimes it seemed to me that it had been a waste of effort, everything I had gone through when escaping from Bolshevist Russia, by crossing, frightened to death, the Finnish border (even if it was by express train and with a prosaic permit), only to pass from one embrace to another almost identical one. Furthermore, Matilda soon began to bore me. She had one constant and, to me, depressing subject of conversation—her husband. This man, she would say, was a noble brute. He would kill her on the spot if he found out. He worshiped her and was savagely jealous. Once in Constantinople he had grabbed an enterprising Frenchman and slapped him several times against the floor, like a rag. He was so passionate, it frightened you. But he was beautiful in his cruelty. I would try to change the subject, but this was Matilda's hobbyhorse, which she straddled with her strong fat thighs. The image she created of her husband was hard to reconcile with the appearance of the man I had hardly noticed; at the same time I found it highly unpleasant to conjecture that perhaps it was not her fantasy at all, and at that moment a jealous fiend in Paris, sensing his predicament, was acting the banal role assigned to him by his wife: gnashing his teeth, rolling his eyes, and breathing heavily through the nose.

Often, as I trudged home, my cigarette case empty, my face burning in the auroral breeze as if I had just removed theatrical make-up, every step sending a throb of pain echoing through my head, I would inspect my puny little bliss from this side and that, and marvel, and pity myself, and feel despondent and afraid. The summit of lovemaking was for me but a bleak knoll with a relentless view. After all, in order to live happily, a man must know now and then a few moments of perfect blankness. Yet I was always exposed, always wide-eyed; even in sleep I did not cease to watch over myself, understanding nothing of my existence, growing crazy at the thought of not being able to stop being aware of myself, and envying all those simple people—clerks, revolutionaries, shopkeepers—who, with confidence and concentration, go about their little jobs. I had no shell of that kind; and on those terrible, pastel-blue mornings, as my heels tapped across the wilderness of the city, I would imagine somebody who goes mad because he begins to perceive clearly the motion of the terrestrial sphere: there he is, staggering, trying to keep his balance, clutching at the furniture; or else settling down in a window seat with an excited grin, like that of the stranger on a train who turns to you with the words: "Really burning up the track, isn't she!" But soon, all the swaying and rocking would make him sick; he would start sucking on a lemon or an ice cube, and lie down flat on the floor, but all in vain. The motion cannot be stopped, the driver is blind, the brakes are nowhere to be found—and his heart would burst when the speed became intolerable.

And how lonely I was! Matilda, who would inquire coyly if I wrote poetry; Matilda, who on the stairs or at the door would artfully incite me to kiss her, only for the opportunity to give a sham shiver and passionately whisper, "You insane boy . . ."; Matilda, of course, did not count. And whom else did I know in Berlin? The secretary of an organization for the assistance of *émigrés;* the family that employed me as tutor; Mr. Weinstock, the owner of a Russian bookshop; the little old German lady from whom I had formerly rented a room—a meager list. Thus, my whole defenseless being invited calamity. One evening the invitation was accepted.

IT was around six. The air indoors was growing heavy with the fall of dusk, and I was barely able to make out the lines of the humorous Chekhov story that I was reading in a stumbling voice to my charges; but I did not dare turn on the lights: those boys had a strange, unchildlike bent for thriftiness, a certain odious housekeeping instinct; they knew the exact prices of sausage, butter, electricity, various makes of cars. As I read aloud *The Double-Bass Romance*, trying vainly to entertain them, and feeling ashamed for myself and for the poor author, I knew they realized my struggle with the blurring dusk and were coolly waiting to see if I would last until the first light came on in the house across the street to set the example. I made it, and light was my reward.

I was just preparing to put greater animation in my voice (at the approach of the most hilarious passage in the story) when suddenly the telephone rang in the hall. We were alone in the flat, and the boys immediately jumped up and raced each other toward the jangling. I remained with the open book in my lap, smiling tenderly at the interrupted line. The call, it turned out, was for me. I sat down in a crackling wicker armchair and put the receiver to my ear. My pupils stood by, one on my right, the other on my left, imperturbably watching me.

"I'm on my way over," said a male voice. "You will be home, I trust?"

"Your trust shall not be betrayed," I answered cheerfully. "But who are you?"

"You don't recognize me? So much the better—it'll be a surprise," said the voice.

"But I'd like to know who is speaking," I insisted, laughing. (Afterward it was only with horror and shame that I could recall the arch playfulness of my tone.)

"In due time," said the voice tersely.

Here I really started to frolic. "But why? Why?" I asked. "What an amusing way to . . ." I realized that I was talking to a vacuum, shrugged, and hung up.

We returned to the parlor. I said, "Now then, where were we?" and, having found the place, resumed reading.

Nevertheless, I felt an odd restlessness. As I read aloud mechanically, I kept wondering who this guest might be. A new arrival from Russia? I vaguely went through the faces and voices I knew—alas, they were not many—and I stopped for some reason at a student named Ushakov. The memory of my single university year in Russia, and of my loneliness there, hoarded this Ushakov like a treasure. When, during a conversation, I would assume a knowing, faintly dreamy expression at the mention of the festive song *"Gaudeamus igitur"* and reckless student days, it meant I was thinking of Ushakov, even though, God knows, I had had only a couple of chats with him (about political or other trifles, I forget what). It was hardly likely, though, that he would be so mysterious over the telephone. I lost myself in conjecture, imagining now a Communist agent, now an eccentric millionaire in need of a secretary.

The doorbell. Again the boys dashed headlong into the hall. I put down my book and strolled after them. With great gusto and dexterity they drew the little steel bolt, fiddled with some additional gadget, and the door opened.

A strange recollection . . . Even now, now that many things have changed, my heart sinks when I summon up that strange recollection, like a dangerous criminal from his cell. It was then that a whole wall of my life crumbled, quite noiselessly, as on the silent screen. I understood that something catastrophic was about to happen, but there was undoubtedly a smile on my face, and, if I am not mistaken, an ingratiating one; and my hand, reaching out, doomed to meet a void, and anticipating that void, nevertheless sought to complete the gesture (associated in my mind with the ring of the phrase "elementary courtesy").

"Down with that hand," were the guest's first words, as he looked at my proffered palm—which was already sinking into an abyss.

No wonder I had not recognized his voice a moment ago. What had come out over the telephone as a certain strained quality distorting a familiar timbre was, in effect, a quite exceptional rage, a thick sound that never until then had I heard in any human voice. That scene remains in my memory like a *tableau vivant*: the brightly lit hall; I, not knowing what to do with my rejected hand; a boy on the right and a boy on the left, both looking not at the visitor but at me; and the visitor himself, in an olive raincoat with fashionable shoulder loops, his face pale as if paralyzed by a photographer's flash—with protruding eyes, dilated nostrils, and a lip replete with venom under the black equilateral triangle of his trimmed mustache. Then began a barely perceptible movement: his lips smacked as they came unstuck, and the thick black cane in his hand twitched slightly; I could no longer take my eyes off that cane.

"What is it?" I asked. "What's the matter? There must be a misunderstanding . . . Surely, a misunderstanding . . ." At this point I found a humiliating, impossible place for my still unaccommodated, still yearning hand: in a vague attempt to retain my dignity, I let my hand rest on the shoulder of one of my pupils; the boy glanced at it askance.

"Look, my good fellow," blurted the visitor, "move away just a bit. I shan't harm them, you don't have to protect them. What I need is some room, because I'm about to beat the dust out of you."

"This is not your house," I said. "You have no right to make a row. I don't understand what you want of me . . ."

He hit me. He caught me a loud, hot crack right on the shoulder, and I lurched to one side from the force of the blow, causing the wicker chair to scuttle out of my way like a live thing. He bared his teeth and got ready to hit me again. The blow landed on my raised arm. Here I retreated and dodged into the parlor. He came after me. Another curious detail: I was shouting at the top of my voice, addressing him by name and patronymic, loudly asking

13

him what I had done to him. When he caught up with me again, I tried to protect myself with a cushion I had grabbed on the run, but he knocked it out of my hand. "This is a disgrace," I shouted. "I'm unarmed. I've been slandered. You'll pay for this . . ." I took refuge behind a table, and as before, everything froze for a moment into a tableau. There he was, teeth bared, cane upraised, and, behind him, on either side of the door, stood the boys: perhaps my memory is stylized at this point, but, so help me, I really believe that one was leaning with folded arms against the wall, while the other sat on the arm of a chair, both imperturbably watching the punishment being administered to me. Presently everything was in motion again, and all four of us passed into the next room; the level of his attack lowered viciously, my hands formed an abject fig leaf, and then, with a horrible blinding blow, he whacked me across the face. How curious that I personally could never bring myself to hit anyone, no matter how badly he might have offended me, and now, under his heavy cane, not only was I unable to strike back (not being versed in the manly arts), but even in those moments of pain and humiliation could not imagine myself raising a hand against a fellow man, especially if that fellow man were angry and strong; nor did I try to escape to my room, where, in a drawer, lay a revolver—acquired, alas, only to frighten off ghosts.

The contemplative immobility of my two pupils, the different poses in which they froze like frescoes at the end of this room or that, the obliging way they turned on the lights the moment I backed into the dark dining room—all this must be a perceptional illusion—disjointed impressions to which I have imparted significance and permanence, and, for that matter, just as arbitrary as the raised knee of a politician stopped by the camera not in the act of dancing a jig but merely in that of crossing a puddle.

In reality, it seems, they were not present throughout my execution; at a certain moment, fearing for their parents' furniture, they dutifully started to phone the police (an attempt that the man cut short by a thunderous roar), but I do not know where to place this moment—at the beginning, or at that apotheosis of suffering and horror when at last I fell limply to the floor, exposing my rounded back to his blows, and kept repeating hoarsely, "Enough, enough, I have a weak heart . . . Enough, I have a weak . . ." My heart, let me remark parenthetically, has always functioned quite well.

A minute later, it was all over. He lit a cigarette, panting loudly and rattling the matchbox; he hung around for a while, appraising matters, and then, saying something about a "little lesson," adjusted his hat and hurried out. I immediately got up from the floor and headed for my room. The boys ran after me. One of them tried to scramble through the door. I hurled him away with a blow of the elbow, and I know it hurt. I locked the door, rinsed my face, nearly crying out from the caustic contact of water, then pulled my suitcase from under the bed and began packing. It was hard—my back ached and my left hand did not work properly.

When I went out into the hall with my coat on, carrying the heavy suitcase, the boys reappeared. I did not even glance at them. As I descended the stairs, I felt them watching me from above, straining over the banisters. A little way down I met their music teacher; Tuesday happened to be her day. She was a meek Russian girl with glasses and bandy legs. I did not greet her but, turning away my swollen face and spurred on by the deathly silence of her surprise, rushed out into the street.

Before committing suicide I wanted to write a few traditional letters and, for five minutes at least, to sit in safety. Therefore I hailed a taxi and went to my former address. Luckily my familiar room was vacant, and the little old landlady started making the bed right away—a wasted effort. I waited impatiently for her to leave, but she fussed on for a long time, filling the pitcher, filling the decanter, drawing the blind, jerking at a stuck cord or something as she looked up, with open black mouth. At last, after emitting a farewell mew, she left.

A wretched, shivering, vulgar little man in a bowler hat stood in the center of the room, for some reason rubbing his hands. That is the glimpse I caught of myself in the mirror. Then I quickly opened the suitcase and took out writing paper and envelopes, found a miserable pencil stub in my pocket, and sat down at the table. It turned out, however, that I had no one to write to. I knew few people and loved no one. So the idea of the letters was discarded, and the rest was discarded too; I had vaguely imagined that I must tidy up things, put on clean linen, and leave all my money—20 marks—in an envelope with a note saying who should receive it. I became aware now that I had decided all this not today but long ago, at various times, when I used to imagine light-heartedly how people went about shooting themselves. Thus a confirmed city dweller who receives an unexpected invitation from a country friend begins by acquiring a flask and a sturdy pair of boots, not because they might actually be needed, but unconsciously, as a consequence of certain former, untested thoughts about the countryside with its long walks through the woods and mountains. But when he arrives, there are no woods and no mountains, nothing but flat farmland, and no one wants to stride along the highway in the heat. I saw now, as one sees a real turnip field instead of the picture-postcard glens and glades, how conventional were my former ideas on presuicidal occupations; a man who has decided upon self-destruction is far removed from mundane affairs, and to sit down and write his will would be, at that moment, an act just as absurd as winding up one's watch, since, together with the man, the whole world is destroyed; the last letter is instantly reduced to dust and, with it, all the postmen; and like smoke, vanishes the estate bequeathed to a nonexistent progeny.

A thing I had long suspected—the world's absurdity—became obvious to me. I suddenly felt unbelievably free, and the freedom itself was an indication of that absurdity. I took the 20-mark note and tore it up into little pieces. I removed my wrist watch and kept dashing it against the floor until it stopped. It occurred to me that, if I wished, I could, at that moment, run out into the street and, with vulgar expletives of lust, embrace any woman I chose; or shoot the first person I met, or smash a store window . . . That was about all I could think of: the imagination of lawlessness has a limited range.

Cautiously, clumsily, I loaded the revolver, then turned off the light. The thought of death, which had once so frightened me, was now an intimate and simple affair. I was afraid, terribly afraid of the monstrous pain the bullet might cause me; but to be afraid of the black velvety sleep, of the even darkness, so much more acceptable and comprehensible than life's motley insomnia? Nonsense—how could one be afraid of *that?* Standing in the middle of the dark room, I unbuttoned my shirt, leaned forward from the hips, felt for and located my heart between the ribs. It was throbbing like a small animal you want to carry to a safe place, a fledgling or field mouse to which you cannot explain that there is nothing to fear, that, on the contrary, you are acting for its own good. But it was so much alive, my heart; I found it somehow repugnant to press the barrel tight against the thin skin under which a portable world was resiliently pulsating, and therefore I drew away my awkwardly bent arm a little, so that the steel would not touch my naked chest. Then I braced myself and fired. There was a strong jolt, and a delightful vibrating sound rang out behind me; that vibration I shall never forget. It was immediately replaced by the warble of water, a throaty gushing noise. I inhaled, and choked on liquidity; everything within me and around me was aflow and astir. I found myself kneeling on the floor; I put out my hand to steady myself but it sank into the floor as into bottomless water.

SOME time later, if one can speak here of time at all, it became clear that after death human thought lives on by momentum. I was tightly swaddled in something—was it a shroud? was it simply taut darkness? I remembered everything—my name, life on earth— with perfect clarity, and found wonderful comfort in the thought that now there was nothing to worry about. With mischievous and carefree logic I progressed from the incomprehensible sensation of tight bandages to the idea of a hospital, and, at once obedient to my will, a spectral hospital ward materialized around me, and I had neighbors, mummies like me, three on either side. What a mighty thing was human thought, that it could hurtle on beyond death! Heaven knows how much longer it would pulsate and create images after my defunct brain had long ceased to be of any use. The familiar crater of a hollow tooth was still with me, and, paradoxically, this afforded some comic relief. I was a bit curious as to how they had buried me, whether there had been a Requiem Mass, and who had come to the funeral.

How persistently, though, and how thoroughly—as if it had been missing its former activity—my thought went about contriving the semblance of a hospital, and the semblance of white-clad human forms moving among the beds, from one of which issued the semblance of human moans. I good-naturedly yielded to these illusions, exciting them, goading them on, until I had managed to create a complete, natural picture, the simple case of a light wound caused by an inaccurate bullet passing clean through the *serratus;* here a doctor (whom I had created) appeared, and hastened to confirm my carefree conjecture. Then, as I was laughingly swearing that I had been clumsily unloading the revolver, my little old lady also appeared, wearing a black straw hat trimmed with cherries. She sat down by my bed, asked how I felt, and, slyly shaking her finger at me, mentioned a pitcher that had been smashed by the bullet . . . oh, how cunningly, in what simple, everyday terms my thought explained the ringing and the gurgling that had accompanied me into nonexistence!

I assumed that the posthumous momentum of my thought would soon play itself out, but apparently, while I was still alive, my imagination had been so fertile that enough of it remained to last for a long time. It went on developing the theme of recovery, and pretty soon had me discharged from the hospital. The restoration of a Berlin street looked a great success—and as I glided off along the sidewalk, delicately trying out my still weak, practically disembodied feet, I thought about everyday matters: that I had to have my watch repaired, and get some cigarettes; and that I had no money. Catching myself with these thoughts— not very alarming ones, for that matter—I vividly evoked the 20-mark note, flesh-colored with an auburn shading, that I had torn up prior to my suicide, and my sensation of freedom and impunity at that moment. Now, however, my action acquired a certain vindictive significance, and I was glad that I had limited myself to a melancholy caprice and had not gone to frolic in the street. For I knew now that after death human thought, liberated from the body, keeps on moving in a sphere where everything is interconnected as before, and has a relative degree of sense, and that a sinner's torment in the afterworld consists precisely in that his tenacious mind cannot find peace until it manages to unravel the complex consequences of his reckless terrestrial actions.

I walked along remembered streets; everything greatly resembled reality, and yet there was nothing to prove that I was not dead and that Passauer Strasse was not a postexistent chimera. I saw myself from the outside, treading water as it were, and was both touched and frightened like an inexperienced ghost watching the existence of a person whose inner lining, inner night, mouth, and taste-in-the-mouth, he knew as well as that person's shape.

My floating mechanical motion brought me to Weinstock's shop. Russian books, instantly printed to humor me, promptly appeared in the window. For a fraction of a second some of the titles still seemed hazy; I focused on them and the haze cleared. The bookshop was empty when I came in, and a cast-iron stove burned in a corner with the dull flame of medieval hells. From somewhere down behind the counter I heard Weinstock's wheezing. "It rolled under," he muttered in a strained voice, "it rolled under." Presently he stood up, and here I caught my imagination (which, it is true, was compelled to work very fast) in an inaccuracy: Weinstock wore a mustache, but now it was not there. My fancy had not finished him in time and the pale space where the mustache should have been showed nothing but a bluish stipple.

"You look awful," he said, by way of greeting. "Shame, shame. What's wrong with you? Been sick?" I answered that I had indeed been ill. "Grippe going around," said Weinstock. "It's been a long time," he went on. "Tell me, did you find a job?"

I answered that for a while I had worked as tutor, but had now lost that position, and that I badly wanted to smoke.

A customer came in and requested a Russian-Spanish dictionary. "I think I have one," said Weinstock, turning toward the shelves and running his finger across the backs of several fat little volumes. "Ah, here's a Russian-Portuguese one—practically the same thing."

"I'll take it," said the customer and left with his useless purchase.

Meanwhile a deep sigh, coming from the back of the store, attracted my attention. Someone, concealed by books, shuffled past with a Russian "och-och-och."

"You've hired an assistant?" I asked Weinstock.

"I'm going to fire him soon," he answered in a low voice. "He's a completely helpless old man. I need someone young."

"And how is the Black Hand doing, Vikentiy Lvovich?"

"If you were not such a malicious skeptic," said Vikentiy Lvovich Weinstock with dignified disapprobation, "I could tell you many interesting things." He was a little hurt, and this was inopportune: my ghostly, impecunious, weightless condition had to be resolved one way or another, but instead my fantasy was producing some rather insipid small talk.

"No, no, Vikentiy Lvovich, why do you call me a skeptic? On the contrary—don't you remember?—this business once cost me good money."

Indeed, when I first met Weinstock, I immediately found in him a kindred trait, a proneness to obsessive ideas. He was convinced that he was being regularly watched by certain persons, to whom he referred, with a mysterious laconism, as "agents." He hinted at the existence of a "black list" on which his name supposedly appeared. I used to tease him, but quaked inwardly. One day, it struck me as odd to run again into a man I had chanced to notice that very morning on the streetcar, an unpleasant blond fellow with shifty eyes—and now there he was, standing on the corner of my street and pretending to read a newspaper. Thenceforth I began to feel uneasy. I would chide myself, and mentally ridicule Weinstock, but I could do nothing about my imagination. At night I would fancy that someone was climbing in through the window. Finally I bought a revolver and calmed down completely. It was to this expenditure (all the more ridiculous, since my firearms license had now been revoked) that I alluded.

"What good will a weapon do you?" he retorted. "They are cunning as the devil. There is only one possible defense against them—brains. My organization—" He suddenly shot me a suspicious glance, as if he had said too much. Here I made up my mind and explained, trying to maintain a jocular manner, that I was in a peculiar situation—no one left to borrow from, yet I still had to live and smoke; and as I said all this, I kept recalling a glib stranger with a missing front tooth who had once presented himself to the mother of my pupils, and, in exactly the same jocular tone, had recounted that he had to go to Wiesbaden that night and was exactly 90 pfennigs short. "Well," she said calmly, "you can keep your Wiesbaden story, but I dare say I'll give you twenty pfennigs. More I cannot, purely as a matter of principle."

However, now, as I indulged in this juxtaposition, I did not feel a bit humiliated. Ever since the shot—that shot which, in my opinion, had been fatal—I had observed myself with curiosity instead of sympathy, and my painful past—before the shot—was now foreign to me. This conversation with Weinstock turned out to be the beginning of a new life for me. In respect to myself I was now an onlooker. My belief in the phantomatic nature of my existence entitled me to certain amusements.

It is silly to seek a basic law, even sillier to find it. Some mean-spirited little man decides that the whole course of humanity can be explained in terms of insidiously revolving signs of the zodiac or as the struggle between an empty and a stuffed belly; he hires a punctilious Philistine to act as Clio's clerk, and begins a wholesale trade in epochs and masses; and then woe to the private individuum, with his two poor u's, hallooing hopelessly amid the dense growth of economic causes. Luckily no such laws exist: a toothache will cost a battle, a drizzle cancel an insurrection. Everything is fluid, everything depends on chance, and all in vain were the efforts of that crabbed bourgeois in Victorian checkered trousers, author of *Das Kapital,* the fruit of insomnia and migraine. There is titillating pleasure in looking back at the past and asking oneself, "What would have happened if . . ." and substituting one chance occurrence for another, observing how, from a gray, barren, humdrum moment in one's life, there grows forth a marvelous rosy event that in reality had failed to flower. A mysterious thing, this branching structure of life: one senses in every past instant a parting of ways, a "thus" and an "otherwise," with innumerable dazzling zigzags bifurcating and trifurcating against the dark background of the past.

All these simple thoughts about the wavering nature of life come to mind when I think how easily I might never have happened to rent a room in the house at 5 Peacock Street, or meet Vanya and her sister, or Roman Bogdanovich, or many other people whom I suddenly found, who started to live all at once, so unexpectedly and unwontedly, around me. And again, had I settled in a different house after my spectral exit from the hospital, perhaps an unimaginable happiness would have become my familiar interlocutor . . . who knows, who knows . . .

Above me, on the top floor, lived a Russian family. I met them through Weinstock, from whom they took books—another fascinating device on the part of the fantasy that directs life. Before actually becoming acquainted, we often met on the stairs, and exchanged somewhat wary glances the way Russians do abroad. I noticed Vanya immediately, and immediately my heart gave a flutter; as when, in a dream, you enter a dream-safe room and find therein, at your dream's disposal, your dream-cornered prey. She had a married sister, Evgenia, a young woman with a nice squarish face that made you think of an amiable and quite handsome bulldog. There was also Evgenia's burly husband. Once, in the downstairs hall, I happened to hold the door for him, and his mispronounced German "thank you" (*danke*) rhymed exactly with the locative case of the Russian word for "bank"—where, by the way, he worked.

With them lived Marianna Nikolaevna, a relative, and, in the evenings, they would have guests, nearly always the same ones. Evgenia was considered the lady of the house. She had a pleasant sense of humor; it was she who had nicknamed her sister "Vanya," when the latter had demanded to be called "Mona Vanna" (after the heroine of some play or other), finding the sound of her real name—Varvara—somehow suggestive of corpulence and pockmarks. It took me a little time to get used to this diminutive of the masculine "Ivan"; gradually, however, it acquired for me the exact shade that Vanya associated with languorous feminine names.

The two sisters resembled each other; the frank bulldogish heaviness of the elder's features was just perceptible in Vanya, but in a different way that lent significance and originality to the beauty of her face. The sisters' eyes, too, were similar—black-brown, slightly asymmetric, and a trifle slanted, with amusing little folds on the dark lids. Vanya's eyes were more opaque at the iris than Evgenia's, and, unlike her sister's, somewhat myopic, as if their beauty made them not quite suitable for everyday use. Both girls were brunettes and wore their hair the same way: a parting in the middle and a big tight bun low on the nape. But the elder's hair did not lie with the same heavenly smoothness, and lacked that precious gloss. I want to shake off Evgenia, get rid of her altogether, so as to have done with the necessity of comparing the sisters; and at the same time I know that if it were not for the resemblance, Vanya's charm would not be quite complete. Only her hands were not elegant: the pale palm contrasted too strongly to the back of the hand, which was very pink and large-knuckled. And there were always little white flecks on her round fingernails.

What further concentration is needed, what added intensity must one's gaze attain, for the brain to enslave the visual image of a person? There they are sitting on the sofa; Evgenia is wearing a black velvet dress, and large beads adorn her white neck; Vanya is in crimson, with small pearls in place of beads; her eyes are lowered under their thick black brows; a dab of powder has not disguised the slight rash on the wide glabella. The sisters wear identical new shoes, and keep glancing at each other's feet—no doubt the same kind of shoe does not look so nice on one's own foot as on that of another. Marianna, a blonde lady doctor with a peremptory voice, is speaking to Smurov and Roman Bogdanovich about the horrors of the recent civil war in Russia. Khrushchov, Evgenia's husband, a jovial gentleman with a fat nose—which he manipulates continually, tugging at it, or getting hold of a nostril and trying to twist it off—is standing in the doorway to the next room, talking with Mukhin, a young man with a pince-nez. The two are facing each other from opposite sides of the doorway, like two atlantes.

Mukhin and the majestic Roman Bogdanovich have long known the family, while Smurov is comparatively a newcomer, although he hardly looks it. None could discern in him the shyness that makes a person so conspicuous among people who know each other well and are bound together by the established echoes of private jokes and by an allusive residue of people's names that to them are alive with special significance, making the newcomer feel as if the magazine story he has started to read had really begun long ago, in old unobtainable issues; and as he listens to the general conversation, rife with references to incidents unknown to him, the outsider keeps silent and shifts his gaze to whoever is speaking, and, the quicker the exchanges, the more mobile become his eyes; but soon the invisible world that lives in the words of the people around him begins to oppress him and he wonders if they have not deliberately contrived a conversation to which he is a stranger. In Smurov's case, however, even if he did occasionally feel left out, he certainly did not show it. I must say that he made a rather favorable impression on me those first evenings. He was not very tall, but well proportioned and dapper. His plain black suit and black bow tie seemed to intimate, in a reserved way, some secret mourning. His pale, thin face was youthful, but the perceptive observer could distinguish in it the traces of sorrow and experience. His manners were excellent. A quiet, somewhat melancholy smile lingered on his lips. He spoke little, but everything he said was intelligent and appropriate, and his infrequent jokes, while too subtle to arouse roars of laughter, seemed to unlock a concealed door in the conversation, letting in an unexpected freshness. One would have thought Vanya could not help liking him immediately because of that noble and enigmatic modesty, that pallor of forehead and slenderness of hand . . . Certain things—for example, the word *"blagodarstvuyte"* ("thank you"), pronounced without the usual slurring, in full, thus retaining its bouquet of conso-nants—were bound to reveal to the perceptive observer that Smurov belonged to the best St. Petersburg society.

Marianna paused for an instant in her account of the horrors of war: she had noticed at last that Roman Bogdanovich, a dignified man with a beard, wanted to put in a word, holding it in his mouth like a large caramel. He had no luck, however, for Smurov was quicker.

"When 'harking to the horrors of the war,' " said Smurov misquoting with a smile from a famous poem, "I feel sorry 'neither for the friend, nor for the friend's mother,' but for those who have never been to war. It is diffi-cult to put into words the musical delight that the singing of bullets gives you . . . Or, when you are flying at full gallop to the attack——"

"War is always hideous," tersely interrupted Marianna. "I must have been brought up dif-ferently from you. A human being who takes another's life is always a murderer, be he an executioner or a cavalry officer."

34

"Personally——" began Smurov, but she interrupted again:

"Military gallantry is a vestige of the past. In my medical practice I have had many occasions to see people who have been crippled or had their lives wrecked by war. Nowadays humanity aspires to new ideals. There is nothing more debasing than to serve as cannon fodder. Perhaps a different upbringing——"

"Personally——" said Smurov.

"A different upbringing," she went on rapidly, "in regard to ideas of humaneness and general cultural interests, makes me look at war through different eyes than you. I have never blazed away at people or driven a bayonet into anyone. Rest assured that among my medical colleagues you will find more heroes than on the battlefield——"

"Personally, I——" said Smurov.

"But enough of this," said Marianna. "I can see neither of us is going to convince the other. The discussion is closed."

A brief silence followed. Smurov sat calmly stirring his tea. Yes, he must be a former officer, a daredevil who liked to flirt with death, and it is only out of modesty that he says nothing about his adventures.

"What I wanted to say was this," boomed Roman Bogdanovich: "You mentioned Constantinople, Marianna Nikolaevna. I had a close friend there among the *émigré* crowd, a certain Kashmarin, with whom I subsequently quarreled, an extremely rough and quick-tempered fellow, even if he did cool off fast and was kind in his own way. Incidentally, he once thrashed a Frenchman nearly to death out of jealousy. Well, he told me the following story. Gives an idea of Turkish mores. Imagine——"

"Thrashed him?" Smurov broke in with a smile. "Oh, good. That's what I like——"

"Nearly to death," repeated Roman Bogdanovich, and launched into his narrative.

Smurov kept nodding approvingly as he listened. He was obviously a person who, behind his unpretentiousness and quietness, concealed a fiery spirit. He was doubtless capable, in a moment of wrath, of slashing a chap into bits, and, in a moment of passion, of carrying a frightened and perfumed girl beneath his cloak on a windy night to a waiting boat with muffled oarlocks, under a slice of honeydew moon, as somebody did in Roman Bogdanovich's story. If Vanya was any judge of character, she must have marked this.

"I have put it all down in detail in my diary," Roman Bogdanovich concluded complacently, and took a swallow of tea.

Mukhin and Khrushchov again froze beside their respective doorjambs; Vanya and Evgenia smoothed kneeward their dresses with an identical stroke; Marianna, for no apparent reason, fixed her gaze on Smurov, who was sitting with his profile toward her and, in keeping with the formula for manly tics, kept tensing his jaw muscles under her unfriendly gaze. I liked him. Yes, I definitely liked him; and I felt that the more intently Marianna, the cultured lady doctor, stared, the more distinct and harmonious became the image of a young daredevil with iron nerves, pale from sleepless nights passed in steppe ravines and shell-shattered railway stations. Everything seemed to be going well.

Vikentiy Lvovich Weinstock, for whom Smurov worked as salesman (having replaced the helpless old man), knew less about him than anyone. There was in Weinstock's nature an attractive streak of recklessness. This is probably why he hired someone he did not know well. His suspiciousness required regular nourishment. Just as there are normal and perfectly decent people who unexpectedly turn out to have a passion for collecting dragonflies or engravings, so Weinstock, a junk dealer's grandson and an antiquarian's son, staid, well-balanced Weinstock who had been in the book business all his life, had constructed a separate little world for himself. There, in the penumbra, mysterious events took place.

India aroused a mystical respect in him: he was one of those people who, at the mention of Bombay, inevitably imagine not a British civil servant, crimson from the heat, but a fakir. He believed in the jinx and the hex, in magic numbers and the Devil, in the evil eye, in the secret power of symbols and signs, and in bare-bellied bronze idols. In the evenings, he would place his hands, like a petrified pianist, upon a small, light, three-legged table. It would start to creak softly, emitting cricketlike chirps, and, having gathered strength, would rise up on one side and then awkwardly but forcefully tap a leg against the floor. Weinstock would recite the alphabet. The little table would follow attentively and tap at the proper letters. Messages came from Caesar, Mohammed, Pushkin, and a dead cousin of Weinstock's. Sometimes the table would be naughty: it would rise and remain suspended in mid-air, or else attack

Weinstock and butt him in the stomach. Weinstock would good-naturedly pacify the spirit, like an animal tamer playing along with a frisky beast; he would back across the whole room, all the while keeping his fingertips on the table waddling after him. For his talks with the dead, he also employed a kind of marked saucer and some other strange contraption with a pencil protruding underneath. The conversations were recorded in special notebooks. A dialog might go thus:

WEINSTOCK: Have you found rest?
LENIN: This is not Baden-Baden.
WEINSTOCK: Do you wish to tell me of life beyond the grave?
LENIN (*after a pause*): I prefer not to.
WEINSTOCK: Why?
LENIN: Must wait till there is a plenum.

A lot of these notebooks had accumulated, and Weinstock used to say that someday he would have the more significant conversations published. Very entertaining was a ghost called Abum, of unknown origin, silly and tasteless, who acted as intermediary, arranging interviews between Weinstock and various dead celebrities. He treated Weinstock with vulgar familiarity.

WEINSTOCK: Who art thou, O Spirit?
REPLY: Ivan Sergeyevich.
WEINSTOCK: Which Ivan Sergeyevich?
REPLY: Turgenev.
WEINSTOCK: Do you continue to create masterpieces?
REPLY: Idiot.
WEINSTOCK: Why do you abuse me?
REPLY (*table convulsed*): Fooled you! This is Abum.

Sometimes when Abum began his horseplay, it was impossible to get rid of him throughout the séance. "He's as bad as a monkey," Weinstock would complain.

Weinstock's partner in these games was a little pink-faced red-haired lady with plump little hands, who smelled of eucalyptus gum, and had always a cold. I learned later that they had been having an affair for a long time, but Weinstock, who in certain respects was singularly frank, never once let this slip out. They addressed each other by their names and patronymics and behaved as though they were merely good friends. She would often drop in at the store and, warming herself by the stove, read a theosophist journal published in Riga. She encouraged Weinstock in his experiments with the hereafter and used to tell how the furniture in her room periodically came to life, how a deck of cards would fly from one spot to another or scatter itself all over the floor, and how once her bedside lamp had hopped down from its table and begun to imitate a dog impatiently tugging at its leash; the plug had finally shot out, there was the sound of a scampering off in the dark, and the lamp was later found in the hall, right by the front door. Weinstock used to say that, alas, real "power" had not been granted him, that his nerves were as slack as old suspenders, while a medium's nerves were practically like the strings of a harp. He did not, however, believe in materialization, and it was only as a curiosity that he preserved a snapshot given him by a spiritualist that showed a pale, pudgy woman with closed eyes disgorging a flowing, cloud-like mass.

He was fond of Edgar Poe and Barbey d'Aurevilly, adventures, unmaskings, prophetic dreams, and secret societies. The presence of Masonic lodges, suicides' clubs, Black Masses, and especially Soviet agents dispatched from "over there" (and how eloquent and awesome was the intonation of that "over there"!) to shadow some poor little *émigré* man, transformed Weinstock's Berlin into a city of wonders amid which he felt perfectly at home. He would hint that he was a member of a large organization, supposedly dedicated to the unraveling and rending of the delicate webs spun by a certain bright-scarlet spider, which Weinstock had had reproduced on a dreadfully garish signet ring giving an exotic something to his hairy hand.

"They are everywhere," he would say with quiet significance. "Everywhere. If I come to a party where there are five, ten, perhaps twenty people, among them, you can be quite sure, oh yes, quite sure, there is at least one agent. I am talking, say, with Ivan Ivanovich, and who can swear that Ivan Ivanovich is to be trusted? Or, say, I have a man working for me in my office—any kind of office, not necessarily this bookstore (I want to keep all personalities out of this, you understand me)—well, how can I know that he is not an agent? They are everywhere, I repeat, everywhere . . . It is such subtle espionage . . . I come to a party, all the guests know each other, and yet there is no

42

guarantee that this very same modest and polite Ivan Ivanovich is not actually . . ." and Weinstock would nod meaningfully.

I soon began to suspect that Weinstock, albeit very guardedly, was alluding to a definite person. Generally speaking, whoever had a chat with him would come away with the impression that Weinstock's target was either Weinstock's interlocutor or a common friend. Most remarkable of all was that once—and Weinstock recalled this occasion with pride— his flair had not deceived him: a person he knew fairly well, a friendly, easygoing, "honest-as-God fellow" (Weinstock's expression), really turned out to be a venomous Soviet sneak. It is my impression that he would be less sorry to let a spy slip away than to miss the chance to hint to the spy that he, Weinstock, had found him out.

Even if Smurov did exhale a certain air of mystery, even if his past did seem rather hazy, was it possible that he . . . ? I see him, for example, behind the counter in his neat black suit, hair combed smooth, with his clean-cut, pale face. When a customer enters, he carefully props his unconsumed cigarette on the edge of the ashtray and, rubbing his slender hands, carefully attends to the needs of the buyer. Sometimes—particularly if the latter is a lady—he smiles faintly, to express either condescension toward books in general, or perhaps raillery at himself in the role of ordinary salesman, and gives valuable advice—this is worth reading, while that is a bit too heavy; here the eternal struggle of the sexes is most entertainingly described, and this novel is not profound but very sparkling, very heady, you know, like champagne. And the lady who has bought the book, the red-lipped lady in the black fur coat, takes away with her a fascinating image: those delicate hands, a little awkwardly picking up the books, that subdued voice, that flitting smile, those admirable manners. At the Khrushchovs', however, Smurov was already beginning to make a somewhat different impression on someone.

The life of this family at 5 Peacock Street was exceptionally happy. Evgenia's and Vanya's father, who spent a large part of the year in London, sent them generous checks, and Khrushchov, too, made excellent money. This, however, was not the point: even had they been penniless, nothing would have changed. The sisters would have been enveloped in the same breeze of happiness, coming from an

unknown direction but felt by even the gloomi-
est and thickest-skinned of visitors. It was as if
they had started on a joyful journey: this top
floor seemed to glide like an airship. One could
not locate exactly the source of that happiness.
I looked at Vanya, and began to think I had
discovered the source . . . Her happiness did
not speak. Sometimes she would suddenly ask
a brief question and, having received the
answer, would immediately fall silent again,
fixing you with her wonder-struck, beautiful,
myopic eyes.

"Where are your parents?" she once asked
Smurov.

"In a very distant churchyard," he answered,
and for some reason made a little bow.

Evgenia, who was tossing a ping-pong ball
in one hand, said she could remember their
mother and Vanya could not. That evening
there was no one besides Smurov and the
inevitable Mukhin: Marianna had gone to a
concert, Khrushchov was working in his room,
and Roman Bogdanovich had stayed at home,
as he did every Friday, to write his diary.
Quiet, prim, Mukhin kept silent, occasionally
adjusting the clip of the rimless pince-nez on
his thin nose. He was very well dressed and
smoked genuine English cigarettes.

Smurov, taking advantage of his silence, suddenly grew more talkative than on previous occasions. Addressing mainly Vanya, he started telling how he had escaped death.

"It happened in Yalta," said Smurov, "when the White Russian troops had already left. I had refused to be evacuated with the others, as I planned to organize a partisan unit and go on fighting the Reds. At first we hid in the hills. During one exchange I was wounded. The bullet passed right through me, just missing my left lung. When I came to, I was lying on my back, and the stars were swimming above me. What could I do? I was bleeding to death, alone in a mountain gorge. I decided to try to make it to Yalta—very risky, but I could not think of any other way. It demanded incredible efforts. I traveled all night, mostly crawling on hands and knees. Finally, at dawn, I got to Yalta. The streets were still fast asleep. Only from the direction of the railway station came the sound of shots. No doubt, somebody was being executed there.

"I had a good friend, a dentist. I went to his house and clapped my hands under the window. He looked out, recognized me, and let me in immediately. I lay in hiding at his place until my wound had healed. He had a young daughter who nursed me tenderly—but that's another story. Obviously, my presence exposed my saviors to dreadful danger, so I was impatient to leave. But where to go? I thought it over and decided to travel north, where it was rumored the civil war had flared up again. So one evening I embraced my kind friend farewell, he gave me some money, which, God willing, I shall repay one day, and here I was, walking once again along the familiar Yalta streets. I had a beard and glasses, and wore an old field jacket. I headed straight for the station. A Red Army soldier was standing at the platform entrance, checking papers. I had a passport bearing the name of Sokolov, army doctor. The Red guard took a look, gave me back the papers, and everything would have gone without a hitch if it hadn't been for a stupid bit of bad luck. Suddenly I heard a woman's voice say, quite calmly, 'He's a White, I know him well.' I kept my wits about me, and made as if to pass through to the platform, without looking around. But I had scarcely walked three paces when a voice, this time a man's, shouted 'Halt!' I halted. Two soldiers and a blowzy female in a military fur cap surrounded me. 'Yes, it's him,' said the woman. 'Take him.' I recognized this Communist as a maid who had formerly worked for some friends of mine. People used to joke that she had a weakness for me, but I had always found her obesity and her carnal lips extremely repulsive. There appeared three more soldiers and a commissar type in semimilitary dress. 'Get moving,' he said. I shrugged and coolly observed that there had been a mistake. 'We'll see about that afterward,' said the commissar.

"I thought they were taking me away to be interrogated. But I soon realized things were a little worse. When we reached the freight warehouse just beyond the station, I was ordered to undress and stand against the wall. I thrust my hand inside my field jacket, pretending to unbutton it, and, in the next instant, had shot down two soldiers with my Browning, and was running for my life. The rest, of course, opened fire on me. A bullet knocked my cap off. I ran around the warehouse, jumped over a fence, shot a man who came at me with a spade, ran up onto the roadbed, dashed across to the other side of the rails in front of an approaching train and, while the long procession of cars separated me from my pursuers, managed to get away."

Smurov went on to tell how, under the cover of night, he had walked to the sea, slept among

some barrels and bags in the port, appropriated
a tin of zwiebacks and a keg of Crimean wine,
and at daybreak, in the auroral mist, set out
alone in a fishing boat, to be rescued after
five days of solitary sail by a Greek sloop. He
spoke in a calm, matter-of-fact, even slightly
monotonous voice, as if talking of trivial matters. Evgenia clucked her tongue sympatheti-
cally; Mukhin listened attentively and sagaci-
ously, every now and then clearing his throat
softly, as if he could not help being deeply
stirred by the narrative and felt respect and
even envy—good, healthy envy—toward a man
who had fearlessly and frankly looked death
in the face. As for Vanya—no, there could be
no more doubt, after this she must fall for
Smurov. How charmingly her lashes punctu-
ated his speech, how delightful was their flutter
of final dots when Smurov finished his tale,
what a glance she cast at her sister—a moist,
sidelong flash—probably to make sure that the
other had not noticed her excitement.

Silence. Mukhin opened his gun-metal cigarette case. Evgenia fussily bethought herself
that it was time to call her husband for tea.
She turned on the threshold and said something inaudible about a cake. Vanya jumped
up from the sofa and ran out too. Mukhin

49

picked up her handkerchief from the floor and laid it carefully on the table.

"May I smoke one of yours?" asked Smurov.

"Certainly," said Mukhin.

"Oh, but you have only one left," said Smurov.

"Go ahead, take it," said Mukhin. "I have more in my overcoat."

"English cigarettes always smell of candied prunes," said Smurov.

"Or molasses," said Mukhin. "Unfortunately," he added in the same tone of voice, "Yalta does not have a railroad station."

This was unexpected and awful. The marvelous soap bubble, bluish, iridescent, with the curved reflection of the window on its glossy side, grows, expands, and suddenly is no longer there, and all that remains is a snitch of ticklish moisture that hits you in the face.

"Before the revolution," said Mukhin, breaking the intolerable silence, "I believe there was a project for a rail link between Yalta and Simferopol. I know Yalta well—been there many times. Tell me, why did you invent all that rigmarole?"

Oh, of course, Smurov could still have saved the situation, still wriggled out of it with some clever new invention, or else, as a last resort,

50

propped up with a good-natured joke what was crumbling with such nauseating speed. Not only did Smurov lose his composure, but he did the worst thing possible. Lowering his voice, he said hoarsely, "Please, I beg you, let this remain between the two of us."

Mukhin obviously felt ashamed for the poor, fantastic fellow; he adjusted his pince-nez and started to say something but stopped short, because at that moment the sisters returned. During tea, Smurov made an agonizing effort to appear gay. But his black suit was shabby and stained, his cheap tie, usually knotted in such a way as to conceal the worn place, tonight exhibited that pitiful tear, and a pimple glowed unpleasantly through the mauve remains of talc on his chin. So that's what it is . . . So it's true after all that there is no riddle to Smurov, that he is but a commonplace babbler, by now unmasked? So that's what it is . . .

No, the riddle remained. One evening, in another house, Smurov's image developed a new and extraordinary aspect, which had previously been only barely perceptible. It was still and dark in the room. A small lamp in the corner was shaded by a newspaper, and this made the ordinary sheet of newsprint acquire a marvelous translucent beauty. And in this penumbra, the conversation suddenly turned to Smurov.

It started with trifles. Fragmentary, vague utterances at first, then persistent allusions to political assassinations in the past, then the terrible name of a famous double agent in old Russia and such separate words as "blood . . . a lot of bother . . . enough . . ." Gradually this autobiographical introduction grew coherent and, after a brief account of a quiet end from a perfectly respectable illness, an odd conclusion to a singularly vile life, the following was spelled out:

"Now this is a warning. Watch out for a certain man. He follows in my footsteps. He spies, he lures, he betrays. He has already been responsible for the death of many. A young *émigré* group is about to cross the border to organize underground work in Russia. But the nets will be set, the group will perish. He spies, lures, betrays. Be on your guard. Watch out for a small man in black. Do not be deceived by his modest appearance. I am telling the truth . . ."

"And who is this man?" asked Weinstock.

The answer was slow in coming.

"Please, Azef, tell us who is this man?"

Under Weinstock's limp fingers, the reversed saucer again moved all over the sheet with the alphabet, dashing hither and thither as it oriented the mark on its rim toward this or that letter. It made six such stops before freezing like a shocked tortoise. Weinstock wrote down and read aloud a familiar name.

"Do you hear?" he said, addressing someone in the darkest corner of the room. "A pretty business! Of course, I need not tell you that I don't believe this for a second. I hope you are not offended. And why should you be offended? It happens quite often at séances that spirits spout nonsense." And Weinstock feigned to laugh it off.

The situation was becoming a curious one. I could already count three versions of Smurov, while the original remained unknown. This occurs in scientific classification. Long ago, Linnaeus described a common species of butterfly, adding the laconic note "*in pratis West-manniae.*" Time passes, and in the laudable pursuit of accuracy, new investigators name the various southern and Alpine races of this common species, so that soon there is not a spot left in Europe where one finds the nominal race and not a local subspecies. Where is the type, the model, the original? Then, at last, a grave entomologist discusses in a detailed paper the whole complex of named races and accepts as the representative of the typical one the almost 200-year-old, faded Scandinavian specimen collected by Linnaeus; and this identification sets everything right.

In the same way I resolved to dig up the true Smurov, being already aware that his image was influenced by the climatic conditions prevailing in various souls—that within a cold soul he assumed one aspect but in a glowing one had a different coloration. I was beginning to enjoy this game. Personally, I viewed Smurov without emotion. A certain bias in his favor that had existed at the outset, had given way to simple curiosity. And yet I experienced an excitement new to me. Just as the scientist does not care whether the color of a wing is pretty or not, or whether its markings are delicate or lurid (but is interested only in its taxonomic characters), I regarded Smurov, without any aesthetic tremor; instead, I found a keen thrill in the classification of Smurovian masks that I had so casually undertaken.

The task was far from easy. For instance, I knew perfectly well that insipid Marianna saw in Smurov a brutal and brilliant officer of the White Army, "the kind that went around stringing people up right and left," as Evgenia informed me in the greatest secrecy during a confidential chat. To define this image accurately, however, I would have had to be familiar with Marianna's entire life, with all the secondary associations that came alive inside her when she looked at Smurov—other reminiscences, other chance impressions and all those lighting effects that vary from soul to soul. My conversation with Evgenia took place soon after Marianna Nikolaevna's departure; it was said she was going to Warsaw, but there were obscure implications of a still more eastwardly journey—perhaps back to the fold; and so Marianna carried away with her and, unless someone sets her right, will preserve to the end of her days, a very particular idea of Smurov.

"And how about you," I asked Evgenia, "what idea have *you* formed?"

"Oh, that's hard to say, all at once," she replied, a smile enhancing both her resemblance to a cute bulldog and the velvety shade of her eyes.

"Please," I insisted.

"In the first place there is his shyness," she

said swiftly. "Yes, yes, a great deal of shyness. I had a cousin, a very gentle, pleasant young man, but whenever he had to confront a crowd of strangers in a fashionable drawing room, he would come in whistling to give himself an independent air—casual and tough at the same time."

"Yes, go on?"

"Let me see, what else is there . . . Sensitivity, I would say, great sensitivity, and, of course, youth; and lack of experience with people . . ."

There was nothing more to be wheedled out of her, and the resulting eidolon was rather pale and not very attractive. It was Vanya's version of Smurov, however, that interested me most of all. I thought about this constantly. I remember how, one evening, chance seemed about to favor me with an answer. I had climbed up from my gloomy room to their sixth-floor apartment only to find both sisters with Khrushchov and Mukhin on the point of leaving for the theater. Having nothing better to do, I went out to accompany them to the taxi stand. Suddenly I noticed that I had forgotten my downstairs key.

"Oh, don't worry, we have two sets," said Evgenia, "you're lucky we live in the same house. Here, you can give them back tomorrow. Good night."

I walked homeward and on the way had a wonderful idea. I imagined a sleek movie villain reading a document he has found on someone else's desk. True, my plan was very sketchy. Smurov had once brought Vanya a yellow, dark-dappled orchid somewhat resembling a frog; now I could ascertain if perhaps Vanya had preserved the cherished remains of the flower in some secret drawer. Once he had brought her a little volume of Gumilyov, the poet of fortitude; it might be worth while checking if the pages had been cut and if the book were lying perhaps on her night table. There was also a photograph, taken with a magnesium flash, in which Smurov had come out magnificently—in semiprofile, very pale, one eyebrow raised—and beside him stood Vanya, while Mukhin skulked in the rear. And, generally speaking, there were many things to discover. Having decided that if I ran into the maid (a very pretty girl, by the way), I would explain that I had come to return the keys, I cautiously unlocked the door of the Khrushchov apartment and tiptoed into the parlor.

It is amusing to catch another's room by surprise. The furniture froze in amazement when I switched on the light. Somebody had left a letter on the table; the empty envelope lay there like an old useless mother, and the little sheet of note paper seemed to be sitting up like a robust babe. But the eagerness, the throb of excitement, the precipitous movement of my hand, all proved uncalled-for. The letter was from a person unknown to me, a certain Uncle Pasha. It contained not a single allusion to Smurov! And if it was coded, then I did not know the key. I flitted over into the dining room. Raisins and nuts in a bowl, and, next to it, spread-eagled and prone, a French novel—the adventures of *Ariane, Jeune Fille Russe.* In Vanya's bedroom, where I went next, it was cold from the open window. I found it so strange to look at the lace bedspread and the altarlike toilet table, where cut glass glistened mystically. The orchid was nowhere to be seen, but in recompense there was the photo propped against the bedside lamp. It had been taken by Roman Bogdanovich. It showed Vanya sitting with luminous legs crossed, behind her was the narrow face of Mukhin, and to Vanya's left, one could make out a black elbow—all that remained of lopped-off Smurov. Shattering evidence! On Vanya's lace-covered pillow there suddenly appeared a star-shaped hollow—the violent imprint of my fist, and in the next moment I was already in the dining room, devouring the raisins and still trembling. Here I remembered the escritoire in the parlor and noiselessly hurried to it. But at this moment the metallic fidgeting of a key sounded from the direction of the front door. I began to retreat hastily, switching off lights as I went, until I found myself in a satiny little boudoir next to the dining room. I fumbled about in the dark, bumped into a sofa and stretched out on it as if I had gone in to take a nap.

In the meantime voices carried from the hall-way—those of the two sisters and that of Khrushchov. They were saying goodbye to Mukhin. Wouldn't he come in for a minute? No, it was late, he would not. Late? Had my disincarnate flitting from room to room really lasted three hours? Somewhere in a theater one had had time to perform a silly play I had seen many times while here a man had but walked through three rooms. Three rooms: three acts. Had I really pondered over a letter in the parlor a whole hour, and a whole hour over a book in the dining room, and an hour again over a snapshot in the strange coolness of the bedroom? . . . My time and theirs had nothing in common.

Khrushchov probably went right to bed; the

sisters entered the dining room alone. The door to my dark damasked lair was not shut tight. I believed that now I would learn all I wanted about Smurov.

". . . But rather exhausting," said Vanya and made a soft och-ing sound conveying to me a yawn. "Give me some root beer, I don't want any tea." There was the light scrape of a chair being moved to the table.

A long silence. Then Evgenia's voice—so close that I cast an alarmed look at the slit of light. ". . . The main thing is, let him tell them his terms. That's the main thing. After all, he speaks English and those Germans don't. I'm not sure I like this fruit paste."

Silence again. "All right, I'll advise him to do that," said Vanya. Something tinkled and fell— a spoon, maybe—and then there was another long pause.

"Look at this," said Vanya with a laugh.

"What's it made of, wood?" asked her sister.

"I don't know," said Vanya and laughed again.

After a while, Evgenia yawned, even more cosily than Vanya.

". . . clock has stopped," she said.

And that was all. They sat on for quite a while; they made clinking sounds with something or other; the nutcracker would crunch and return to the tablecloth with a thump; but there was no more talk. Then the chairs moved again. "Oh, we can leave it there," drawled Evgenia languidly, and the magical slit from which I had expected so much was abruptly extinguished. Somewhere a door slammed, Vanya's faraway voice said something, by now unintelligible, and then followed silence and darkness. I lay on the sofa for a while longer and suddenly noticed that it was already dawn. Whereupon I cautiously made my way to the staircase and returned to my room.

I imagined rather vividly Vanya protruding the tip of her tongue at one side of her mouth and snipping off with her little scissors the unwanted Smurov. But maybe it was not so at all: sometimes something is cut off in order to be framed separately. And to confirm this last conjecture, a few days later Uncle Pasha quite unexpectedly arrived from Munich. He was going to London to visit his brother and stayed in Berlin only a couple of days. The old goat had not seen his nieces for a very long time and was inclined to recall how he used to place sobbing Vanya across his knee and spank her. At first sight this Uncle Pasha seemed merely three times her age but one had only to look a little closer and he deteriorated under your very eyes. In point of fact, he was not 50 but 80, and one could imagine nothing more dreadful than this mixture of youthfulness and decrepitude. A jolly corpse in a blue suit, with dandruff on his shoulders, clean-shaven, with bushy eyebrows and prodigious tufts in his nostrils, Uncle Pasha was mobile, noisy and inquisitive. At his first appearance he interrogated Evgenia in a sprayey whisper about every guest, quite openly pointing now at this person, now at that, with his index, which ended in a yellow, monstrously long nail. On the following day occurred one of those coincidences involving new arrivals that for some reason are so frequent, as if there existed some tasteless prankish Fate not unlike Weinstock's Abum who, on the very day you return home from a journey, has you meet the man who had chanced to be sitting opposite you in the railway car. For several days already I had felt a strange discomfort in my bullet-punctured chest, a sensation resembling a draft in a dark room. I went to see a Russian doctor, and there, sitting in the waiting room, was of course Uncle Pasha. While I was debating whether or not to accost him (assuming that since the previous evening he had had time to forget both my face and my name), this decrepit prattler, loath to keep hidden a single grain from the storage bins of his experience, started a conversation with an elderly lady who did not know him, but who was evidently fond of openhearted strangers. At first I did not follow their talk, but suddenly Smurov's name gave me a jolt. What I learned from Uncle Pasha's pompous and trite words was so important that when he finally disappeared behind the doctor's door, I left immediately without waiting my turn—and did so quite automatically, as if I had come to the doctor's office only to hear Uncle Pasha: now the performance was over and I could leave. "Imagine," Uncle Pasha had said, "the baby girl blossomed into a genuine rose. I'm an expert in roses and concluded at once that there must be a young man in the picture. And then her sister says to me, 'It's a great secret, Uncle, so don't tell anyone, but she's been in love with this Smurov for a long time.' Well, of course, it's none of my business. One Smurov is no worse than another. But it really gives me a kick to think that there was a time when I used to give that lassie a good spanking on her bare little buttocks, and now there she is, a bride. She simply worships

63

him. Well, that's the way it is, my good lady, we've had our fling, now let the others have theirs . . ."

So—it has happened. Smurov is loved. Evidently Vanya, myopic but sensitive Vanya, had discerned something out of the ordinary in Smurov, had understood something about him, and his quietness had not deceived her. That same evening, at the Khrushchovs', Smurov was particularly quiet and humble. Now, however, when one knew what bliss had smitten him—yes, smitten (for there is bliss so strong that, with its blast, with its hurricane howl, it resembles a cataclysm)—now a certain palpitation could be discerned in his quietude, and the carnation of joy showed through his enigmatic pallor. And dear God, how he gazed at Vanya! She would lower her lashes, her nostrils would quiver, she would even bite her lips a little, hiding from all her exquisite feelings. That night it seemed that something must be resolved.

Poor Mukhin was not there: he had gone for a few days to London. Khrushchov was also absent. In compensation, however, Roman Bogdanovich (who was gathering material for the diary which with old-maidish precision he

64

weekly sent to a friend in Tallin) was more than ever his sonorous and importunate self. The sisters sat on the sofa as always. Smurov stood leaning one elbow on the piano, ardently gazing at the smooth parting in Vanya's hair, at her dusky-red cheeks . . . Evgenia several times jumped up and thrust her head out of the window—Uncle Pasha was coming to say goodbye and she wanted to be sure and be on hand to unlock the elevator for him. "I adore him," she said, laughing. "He is such a character. I bet he won't let us accompany him to the station."

"Do you play?" Roman Bogdanovich politely asked Smurov, with a meaningful look at the piano. "I used to play once," Smurov calmly replied. He opened the lid, glanced dreamily at the bared teeth of the keyboard, and brought the lid back down. "I love music," Roman Bogdanovich observed confidentially. "I recall, in my student days——"

"Music," said Smurov in a louder tone, "good music at least, expresses that which is inexpressible in words. Therein lie the meaning and the mystery of music."

"There he is," shouted Evgenia and left the room.

"And you, Varvara?" asked Roman Bogdanovich in his coarse, thick voice. "You—'with fingers lighter than a dream'—eh? Come on, anything . . . Some little ritornello." Vanya shook her head and seemed about to frown but instead giggled and lowered her face. No doubt, what excited her mirth was this thick-head's inviting her to sit down at the piano when her soul was ringing and flowing with its own melody. At this moment one could have noted in Smurov's face a most violent desire that the elevator carrying Evgenia and Uncle Pasha get stuck forever, that Roman Bogdanovich tumble right into the jaws of the blue Persian lion depicted on the rug, and, most important, that I—the cold, insistent, tire-less eye—disappear.

Meanwhile Uncle Pasha was already blow-ing his nose and chuckling in the hall; now he came in and paused on the threshold, smiling foolishly and rubbing his hands. "Evgenia," he said, "I'm afraid I don't know anybody here. Come, make the introductions."

"Oh, my goodness!" said Evgenia. "It's your own niece!"

"So it is, so it is," said Uncle Pasha and added something outrageous about cheeks and peaches.

"He probably won't recognize the others

either," sighed Evgenia and began introducing us in a loud voice.

"Smurov!" exclaimed Uncle Pasha, and his eyebrows bristled. "Oh, Smurov and I are old friends. Happy, happy man," he went on mischievously, palpating Smurov's arms and shoulders. "And you think we don't know . . . We know all about it . . . I'll say one thing—take good care of her! She is a gift from heaven. May you be happy, my children . . ."

He turned to Vanya but she, pressing a crumpled handkerchief to her mouth, ran out of the room. Evgenia, emitting an odd sound, hurried off after her. Yet Uncle Pasha did not notice that his careless babbling, intolerable to a sensitive being, had driven Vanya to tears. Eyes bulging, Roman Bogdanovich peered with great curiosity at Smurov, who—whatever his feelings—maintained an impeccable composure.

"Love is a great thing," said Uncle Pasha, and Smurov smiled politely. "This girl is a treasure. And you, you're a young engineer, aren't you? Your job coming along well?"

Without going into details Smurov said he was doing all right. Roman Bogdanovich suddenly slapped his knee and grew purple.

"I'll put in a good word for you in London,"

Uncle Pasha said. "I have many connections. Yes, I'm off, I'm off. Right now, as a matter of fact."

And the astounding old fellow glanced at his watch and proffered us both hands. Smurov, overcome with love's bliss, unexpectedly embraced him.

"How do you like that? . . . There is a queer one for you!" said Roman Bogdanovich, when the door had closed behind Uncle Pasha.

Evgenia came back into the parlor. "Where is he?" she asked with surprise: there was something magical about his disappearance.

She hastened up to Smurov. "Please, excuse my uncle," she began. "I was foolish enough to tell him about Vanya and Mukhin. He must have got the names mixed up. At first I did not realize how gaga he was——"

"And I listened and thought I was going crazy," Roman Bogdanovich put in, spreading his hands.

"Oh, come on, come on, Smurov," Evgenia went on. "What's the matter with you? You must not take it to heart like that. After all, it's no insult to you."

"I'm all right, I just did not know," Smurov said hoarsely.

"What do you mean you did not know?

Everybody knows . . . It's been going on for ages. Yes, of course, they adore each other. It's almost two years now. Listen, I'll tell you something amusing about Uncle Pasha: once, when he was still relatively young—no, don't you turn away, it's a very interesting story—one day, when he was relatively young he happened to be walking along Nevski Avenue——"

There follows a brief period when I stopped watching Smurov: I grew heavy, surrendered again to the gnawing of gravity, donned anew my former flesh, as if indeed all this life around me was not the play of my imagination, but was real, and I was part of it, body and soul. If you are not loved, but do not know for sure whether a potential rival is loved or not, and, if there are several, do not know which of them is luckier than you; if you subsist on that hopeful ignorance which helps you to resolve in conjecture an otherwise intolerable agitation; then all is well, you can live. But woe when the name is at last announced, and that name is not yours! For she was so enchanting, it even brought tears to one's eyes, and, at the merest thought of her, a moaning, awful, salty night would well up within me. Her downy face, nearsighted eyes and tender unpainted lips, which grew chapped and a little swollen from the cold, and whose color seemed to run at the edges, dissolving in a feverish pink that seemed to need so badly the balm of a butterfly kiss; her short bright dresses: her big knees, which squeezed together, unbearably tight, when she played skat with us, bending her silky black head over her cards; and her hands, adolescently clammy and a little coarse, which one especially longed to touch and kiss—yes, everything about her was excruciating and somehow irremediable, and only in my dreams, drenched with tears, did I at last embrace her and feel under my lips her neck and the hollow near the clavicle. But she would always break away, and I would awaken, still throbbing. What difference did it make to me whether she were stupid or intelligent, or what her childhood had been like, or what books she read, or what she thought about the universe? I really knew nothing about her, blinded as I was by that burning loveliness which replaces everything else and justifies everything, and which, unlike a human soul (often accessible and possessable), can in no way be appropriated, just as one cannot include among one's belongings the colors of ragged sunset clouds above black houses, or a flower's smell that one inhales endlessly, with tense nostrils, to the point of intoxication, but cannot draw completely out of the corolla.

Once, at Christmas, before a ball to which they were all going without me, I glimpsed, in a strip of mirror through a door left ajar, her sister powdering Vanya's bare shoulder blades; on another occasion I noticed a flimsy bra in the bathroom. For me these were exhausting events, that had a delicious but dreadfully draining effect on my dreams, although never once in them did I go beyond a hopeless kiss (I myself do not know why I always wept so when we met in my dreams). What I needed from Vanya I could never have taken for my perpetual use and possession anyway, as one cannot possess the tint of the cloud or the scent of the flower. Only when I finally realized that my desire was bound to remain insatiable and that Vanya was wholly a creation of mine, did I calm down, and grow accustomed to my own excitement, from which I had extracted all the sweetness that a man can possibly obtain from love.

Gradually my attention returned to Smurov. Incidentally, it turned out that, in spite of his interest in Vanya, Smurov had, on the sly, set his sights on the Khrushchovs' maid, a girl of 18, whose special attraction was the sleepy cast of her eyes. She herself was anything but sleepy. It is amusing to think what depraved devices of love play this modest-looking girl—named Gretchen or Hilda, I do not remember which—would think up when the door was locked and the practically naked light bulb, suspended by a long cord, illumined the photograph of her fiancé (a sturdy fellow in a Tirolese hat) and an apple from the masters' table. These doings Smurov recounted in full detail, and not without a certain pride, to Weinstock, who abhorred indecent stories and would emit a strong eloquent "Pfui!" upon hearing something salacious. And that is why people were especially eager to tell him things of this nature.

Smurov would reach her room by the back stairs, and stay with her a long time. Apparently, Evgenia once noticed something—a quick scuttle at the end of the corridor, or muffled laughter behind the door—for she mentioned with irritation that Hilda (or Gretchen) had taken up with some fireman. During this outburst Smurov cleared his throat complacently a few times. The maid, casting down her charming dim eyes, would pass through the dining room; slowly and carefully place a bowl of fruit and her breasts on the sideboard; sleepily pause to brush back a dim fair lock off her temple, and then somnambule back to the kitchen; and Smurov would rub his hands together as if about to deliver a speech, or smile in the wrong places during the general conversation. Weinstock would grimace and spit in disgust when Smurov dwelt on the pleasure of watching the prim servant maid at work when, such a short time ago, gently pattering with bare feet on the bare floor, he had been fox-trotting with the creamy-haunched wench in her narrow little room to the distant sound of a phonograph coming from the masters' quarters: Mister Mukhin had brought back from London some really lovely records of moan-sweet Hawaiian dance music.

"You're an adventurer," Weinstock would say, "a Don Juan, a Casanova . . ." To himself, however, he undoubtedly called Smurov a double or triple agent and expected the little table within which fidgeted the ghost of Azef to yield important new revelations. This image of Smurov, though, interested me but little now: it was doomed to gradual fading owing to the absence of supporting evidence. The mystery of Smurov's personality, of course, remained, and one could imagine Weinstock, several years hence and in another city, mentioning, in passing, a strange man who had once worked as a salesman for him, and who now was God knows where. "Yes, a very odd character," Weinstock will say pensively. "A man knit of incomplete intimations, a man with a secret hidden in him. He could ruin a girl . . . Who had sent him, and whom he was trailing, it is hard to say. Though I did learn from one reliable source . . . But then I don't want to say anything."

Much more entertaining was Gretchen's (or Hilda's) concept of Smurov. One day in January a new pair of silk stockings disappeared from Vanya's wardrobe, whereupon everyone remembered a multitude of other petty losses: 70 pfennigs in change left on the table and huffed like a piece in checkers: a crystal powder box that "escaped from the Nes S. S. R.," as Khrushchov punned; a silk handkerchief, much treasured for some reason ("Where on earth could I have put it?"). Then, one day, Smurov came wearing a bright-blue tie with a peacock sheen, and Khrushchov blinked and said that he used to have a tie just exactly like that; Smurov grew absurdly embarrassed, and he never wore that tie again. But, of course, it did not enter anyone's head that the silly goose had stolen the tie (she used to say, by the way, "A tie is a man's best ornament") and had given it, out of sheer mechanical habit, to her boyfriend of the moment—as Smurov bitterly informed Weinstock. Her undoing came when Evgenia happened to enter her room while she was out, and found in the dresser a collection of familiar articles resurrected from the dead. And so Gretchen (or Hilda) left for an unknown destination; Smurov tried to locate her but soon gave up and confessed to Weinstock that enough was enough. That evening Evgenia said she had learned some remarkable things from the janitor's wife. "It was not a fireman, it was not a fireman at all," said Evgenia, laughing, "but a foreign poet, isn't that delightful? . . . This foreign poet had had a tragic love affair and a family estate the size of Germany, but he was forbidden to return home, really delightful, isn't it? . . . It's a pity the janitor's wife didn't ask what his name was—I'm sure he was Russian, and I wouldn't even be surprised if it were someone who comes to see us . . . For instance, that chap last year, you know whom I mean—the dark boy with the fatal charm, what was his name?"

"I know whom you have in mind," Vanya put in. "That baron something or other."

"Or maybe it was somebody else," Evgenia went on. "Oh, that's *so* delightful! A gentleman who was all soul, a 'spiritual gentleman,' says the janitor's wife. I could die laughing . . ."

"I'll make a point of taking all that down," said Roman Bogdanovich in a juicy voice. "My friend in Tallin will get a most interesting letter."

"Don't you ever get tired of it?" asked Vanya. "I started keeping a diary several times but always dropped it. And when I read it over I was always ashamed of what I had put down."

"Oh, no," said Roman Bogdanovich. "If you do it thoroughly and regularly you get a good feeling, a feeling of self-preservation, so to speak—you preserve your entire life, and, in later years, rereading it, you may find it not devoid of fascination. For instance, I've done a description of you that would be the envy of any professional writer. A stroke here, a stroke there, and there it is—a complete portrait . . ."

"Oh, please show me!" said Vanya.

"I can't," Roman Bogdanovich answered with a smile.

"Then show it to Evgenia," said Vanya.

"I can't. I'd like to, but I can't. My Tallin friend stores up my weekly contributions as they arrive, and I deliberately keep no copies so there will be no temptation to make changes ex post facto—to cross things out and so on. And one day, when Roman Bogdanovich is very old, Roman Bogdanovich will sit down at his desk and start rereading his life. That's who I'm writing for—for the future old man with the Santa-Claus beard. And if I find that my life has been rich and worth while, then I shall leave this memoir as a lesson for posterity."

"And if it's all nonsense?" asked Vanya.

"What is nonsense to one may have sense for another," replied Roman Bogdanovich rather sourly.

The thought of this epistolary diary had long interested and somewhat troubled me. Gradually the desire to read at least one excerpt became a violent torment, a constant preoccupation. I had no doubt that those jottings contained a description of Smurov. I knew that very often a trivial account of conversations, and country rambles and one's neighbor's tulips or parrots, and what one had for lunch that overcast day when, for example, the king was beheaded—I knew that such trivial notes often live hundreds of years, and that one reads them with pleasure, for the savor of anciency, for the name of a dish, for the festive-looking spaciousness where now tall buildings crowd together. And, besides, it often happens that the diarist, who in his lifetime has gone unnoticed or had been ridiculed by forgotten nonentities, emerges 200 years later as a first-rate writer, who knew how to immortalize, with a striggle of his old-fashioned pen, an airy landscape, the smell of a stagecoach, or the oddities of an acquaintance. At the very thought that Smurov's image might be so securely, so lastingly preserved I felt a sacred chill, I grew crazed with desire, and felt that I must at any cost interpose myself spectrally between Roman Bogdanovich and his friend in Tallin. Experience warned me, of course, that the particular image of Smurov, which was perhaps destined to live forever (to the delight of scholars), might be a shock to me; but the urge to gain possession of this secret, to see Smurov through the eyes of future centuries, was so bedazzling that no thought of disappointment could frighten me. I feared only one thing—a lengthy and meticulous perlustration, since it was difficult to imagine that in the very first letter I intercepted, Roman Bogdanovich would start right off (like the voice, in full swing, that bursts upon your ears when you turn on the radio for a moment) with an eloquent report on Smurov.

I recall a dark street on a stormy March night. The clouds rolled across the sky, assuming various grotesque attitudes like staggering and ballooning buffoons in a hideous carnival, while, hunched up in the blow, holding onto my derby which I felt would explode like a bomb if I let go of its brim, I stood by the house where lived Roman Bogdanovich. The only witnesses to my vigil were a street light that seemed to blink because of the wind, and a sheet of wrapping paper that now scurried along the sidewalk, now attempted with odious friskiness to wrap itself around my legs, no matter how hard I tried to kick it away. Never before had I experienced such a wind or seen such a drunken, disheveled sky. And this irked me. I had come to spy on a ritual—Roman Bogdanovich, at midnight between Friday and Saturday, depositing a letter in the mailbox— and it was essential that I see it with my own eyes before I begin developing the vague plan I had conceived. I hoped that as soon as I saw Roman Bogdanovich struggling with the wind for possession of the mailbox, my bodiless plan would immediately grow alive and distinct (I was thinking of rigging up an open sack which I would somehow introduce into the mailbox, placing it in such a way that a letter dropped into the slot would fall into my net). But this wind—now humming under the dome of my headgear, now inflating my trousers, or clinging to my legs until they seemed skeletal—was in my way, preventing me from concentrating on the matter. Midnight would soon close completely the acute angle of time; I knew that Roman Bogdanovich was punctual. I looked at the house and tried to guess behind which of the three or four lighted windows there sat at this very moment a man, bent over a sheet of paper, creating an image, perhaps immortal, of Smurov. Then I would shift my gaze to the dark cube fixed to the cast-iron railing, to that dark mailbox into which presently an unthinkable letter would sink, as into eternity. I stood away from the street light; and the shadows afforded me a kind of hectic protection. Suddenly a yellow glow appeared in the glass of the front door, and in my excitement I loosened my grip on the brim of my hat. In the next instant I was gyrating on one spot, both hands raised, as if the hat just snatched from me were still flying around my head. With a light thump, the derby fell and rolled away on the sidewalk. I dashed in pursuit, trying to step on the thing to stop it—and almost collided on the run with Roman Bogdanovich, who picked up my hat with one hand, while holding with the other a sealed envelope that looked white and enormous. I think my appearance in his neighborhood at that late hour puzzled him. For a moment the wind enveloped us in its violence; I yelled a greeting, trying to out-shout the din of the demented night, and then, with two fingers, lightly and neatly plucked the letter from Roman Bogdanovich's hand. "I'll mail it, I'll mail it," I shouted. "It's on my way, it's on my way . . ." I had time to glimpse an expression of alarm and uncertainty on his face, but I immediately made off, running the 20 yards to the mailbox into which I pretended to thrust something, but instead squeezed the letter into my inside breast pocket. Here he overtook me. I noticed his carpet slippers. "What manners you have," he said with displeasure. "Perhaps I had no intention to post it. Here, take this hat of yours . . . Ever see such a wind? . . ."

"I'm in a hurry," I gasped (the swift night took my breath away). "Goodbye, goodbye!" My shadow, as it plunged into the aura of the street lamp, stretched out and passed me, but then was lost in the darkness. No sooner had I left that street, than the wind ceased; all was startlingly still, and amid the stillness a street-car was groaning around a turn.

I hopped on it without glancing at its number, for what lured me was the festive brightness of its interior, since I had to have light immediately. I found a cozy corner seat, and with furious haste ripped open the envelope. Here someone came up to me and, with a start, I placed my hat over the letter. But it was only the conductor. Feigning a yawn, I calmly paid for my ticket, but kept the letter concealed all the time, so as to be safe from possible testimony in court—there is nothing more damning than those inconspicuous witnesses, conductors, taxi drivers, janitors. He went away and I unfolded the letter. It was ten pages long, in a round hand and without a single correction. The beginning was not very interesting. I skipped several pages and suddenly, like a familiar face amid a hazy crowd, there was Smurov's name. What amazing luck!

"I propose, my dear Fyodor Robertovich, to return briefly to that rascal. I fear it may bore you, but, in the words of the Swan of Weimar—I refer to the illustrious Goethe—(there followed a German phrase). Therefore allow me to dwell on Mr. Smurov again and treat you to a little psychological study . . ."

I paused and looked up at a milk chocolate advertisement with lilac alps. This was my last chance to renounce penetrating into the secret of Smurov's immortality. What did I care if this letter would indeed travel across a remote mountain pass into the next century, whose very designation—a two and three zeros—is so fantastic as to seem absurd? What did it matter to me to what kind of portrait a long-dead author would "treat," to use his own vile expression, his unknown posterity? And anyway, was it not high time to abandon my enterprise, to call off the hunt, the watch, the insane attempt to corner Smurov? But alas, this was mental rhetoric: I knew perfectly well that no force on earth could prevent me from reading that letter.

"I have the impression, dear friend, that I have already written you of the fact that

Smurov belongs to that curious class of people I once called 'sexual lefties.' Smurov's entire appearance, his frailness, his decadence, his mincing gestures, his fondness for Eau de Cologne, and, in particular, those furtive, passionate glances that he constantly directs toward your humble servant—all this has long since confirmed this conjecture of mine. It is remarkable that these sexually unfortunate individuals, while yearning physically for some handsome specimen of mature virility, often choose for object of their (perfectly platonic) admiration—a woman—a woman they know well, slightly, or not at all. And so Smurov, notwithstanding his perversion, has chosen Varvara as his ideal. This comely but rather stupid lass is engaged to a certain M. M. Mukhin, one of the youngest colonels in the White Army, so Smurov has full assurance that he will not be compelled to perform that which he is neither capable nor desirous of performing with any lady, even if she were Cleopatra herself. Furthermore, the 'sexual lefty'—I admit I find the expression exceptionally apt—frequently nurtures a tendency to break the law, which infraction is further facilitated for him by the fact that an infraction of the law of nature is already there. Here again our friend Smurov is no exception. Imagine, the other day Filip Innokentievich Khrushchov confided to me that Smurov was a thief, a thief in the ugliest sense of the word. My interlocutor, so it turned out, had handed him a silver snuffbox with occult symbols—an object of great age—and had asked him to show it to an expert. Smurov took this beautiful antique and the next day announced to Khrushchov with all the outward signs of dismay that he had lost it. I listened to Khrushchov's account and explained to him that sometimes the urge to steal is a purely pathological phenomenon, even having a scientific name—kleptomania. Khrushchov, like many pleasant but limited people, began naïvely denying that in the present instance we are dealing with a 'kleptomaniac' and not a criminal. I did not set forth certain arguments that would undoubtedly have convinced him. To me everything is clear as day. Instead of branding Smurov with the humiliating designation of 'thief,' I am sincerely sorry for him, paradoxical as it may seem.

"The weather has changed for the worse, or, rather, for the better, for are not this slush and wind harbingers of spring, pretty little spring, which, even in an elderly man's heart, arouses vague desires? An aphorism comes to mind that will doubtless——"

I skimmed to the end of the letter. There was nothing further of interest to me. I cleared my throat and with untrembling hands tidily folded the sheets.

"Terminal stop, sir," a gruff voice said over me.

Night, rain, the outskirts of the city . . .

Dressed in a remarkable fur coat with a feminine collar, Smurov is sitting on a step of the staircase. Suddenly Khrushchov, also in fur, comes down and sits next to him. It is very difficult for Smurov to begin, but there is little time, and he must take the plunge. He frees a slender hand sparkling with rings—rubies, all rubies—from the ample fur sleeve and, smoothing his hair, says, "There is something of which I want to remind you, Filip Innokentievich. Please listen carefully."

Khrushchov nods. He blows his nose (he has a bad cold from constantly sitting on the stairs). He nods again, and his swollen nose twitches.

Smurov continues, "I am about to speak of

a small incident that occurred recently. Please listen carefully."

"At your service," replies Khrushchov.

"It is difficult for me to begin," says Smurov. "I might betray myself by an incautious word. Listen carefully. Listen to me, please. You must understand that I return to this incident without any particular thought at the back of my mind. It would not even enter my head that you should think me a thief. You yourself must agree with me that I cannot possibly know of your thinking this—after all, I don't read other people's letters. I want you to understand that the subject has come up quite by chance . . . Are you listening?"

"Go on," says Khrushchov, snuggling in his fur.

"Good. Let us think back, Filip Innokentievich. Let us recall the silver miniature. You asked me to show it to Weinstock. Listen carefully. As I left you I was holding it in my hand. No, no, please don't recite the alphabet. I can communicate with you perfectly well without the alphabet. And I swear, I swear by Vanya, I swear by all the women I have loved, I swear that every word of the person whose name I cannot utter—since otherwise you will

think I read other people's mail, and am therefore capable of thievery as well—I swear that
every word of his is a lie: I really did lose it.
I came home, and I no longer had it, and it is
not my fault. It is just that I am very absent-
minded, and love her so much."

But Khrushchov does not believe Smurov; he
shakes his head. In vain does Smurov swear, in
vain does he wring his white, glittering hands—
it is no use, words to convince Khrushchov do
not exist. (Here my dream exhausted its
meager supply of logic: by now the staircase
on which the conversation took place was
standing all by itself in open country, and below there were terraced gardens and the haze
of trees in blurry bloom; the terraces stretched
away into the distance, where one seemed to
distinguish cascades and mountain meadows.)
"Yes, yes," said Khrushchov in a hard menac-
ing voice. "There was something inside that
box, therefore it is irreplaceable. Inside it was
Vanya—yes, yes, this happens sometimes to
girls . . . A very rare phenomenon, but it happens, it happens . . ."

I awoke. It was early morning. The window-
panes were trembling from a passing truck.
They had long ceased to be frosted with a
mauve film, for spring was near. I paused to

think how much had happened lately, how many new people I had met, and how enthralling, how hopeless was this house-to-house search, this quest of mine for the real Smurov. There is no use to dissemble—all these people I met were not live beings but only chance mirrors for Smurov; one among them, though, and for me the most important, the brightest mirror of all, still would not yield me Smurov's reflection. Hosts and guests at 5 Peacock Street move before me from light to shade, effortlessly, innocently, created merely for my amusement. Once again Mukhin, rising slightly from the sofa, stretches his hand across the table toward the ashtray, but I see neither his face, nor that hand with the cigarette; I see only his other hand, which (already unconsciously!) rests momentarily on Vanya's knee. Once again Roman Bogdanovich, bearded and with a pair of red apples for cheeks, bends his congested face to blow on the tea, and again Marianna sits down and crosses her legs, thin legs in apricot-colored stockings. And, as a joke—it was Christmas Eve, I think—Khrushchov pulls on his wife's fur coat, assumes mannequin attitudes before the mirror, and walks about the room to general laughter, which gradually begins to grow forced, because Khrushchov always overdoes his jokes. Evgenia's lovely little hand, with its nails so glossy they seem moist, picks up a table-tennis paddle, and the little celluloid ball pings dutifully back and forth across the green net. Again in the semidarkness Weinstock floats by, seated at his planchette table as if at a steering wheel; again the maid—Hilda or Gretchen—passes dreamily from one door to another, and suddenly begins to whisper and wriggle out of her dress. Whenever I wish, I can accelerate or retard to ridiculous slowness the motions of all these people, or distribute them in different groups, or arrange them in various patterns, lighting them now from below, now from the side . . . For me, their entire existence has been merely a shimmer on a screen.

But wait, life did make one last attempt to prove to me that it was real—oppressive and tender, provoking excitement and torment, possessed of blinding possibilities for happiness, with tears, with a warm wind.

That day I climbed up to their flat at noon. I found the door unlocked, the rooms empty, the windows open. Somewhere a vacuum cleaner was putting its whole heart into an ardent whir. All at once, through the glass door leading from the parlor to the balcony, I saw Vanya's bowed head. She was sitting on the balcony with a book and—strangely enough—this was the first time I found her at home alone. Ever since I had been trying to subdue my love by telling myself that Vanya, like all the others, existed only in my imagination, and was a mere mirror, I had got into the habit of assuming a special jaunty tone with her, and now, greeting her, I said, without the least embarrassment, that she was "like a princess welcoming spring from her lofty tower." The balcony was quite small, with empty green flower boxes, and, in one corner, a broken clay pot, which I mentally compared to my heart, since it often happens that one's style of speaking to a person affects one's way of thinking in that person's presence. The day was warm, though not very sunny, with a touch of turbidity and dampness—diluted sunlight and a tipsy but meek little breeze, fresh from a visit to some public garden where the young grass was already nappy and green against the black of the loam. I took a breath of this air, and realized simultaneously that Vanya's wedding was only a week away. This thought brought back all the yearn and ache, I forgot again about

Smurov, forgot that I must talk in a carefree manner. I turned away and began looking down at the street. How high we were, and so completely alone. "He will be quite a while yet," said Vanya. "They keep you waiting for hours in those offices."

"Your romantic vigil . . ." I began, compelling myself to maintain that lifesaving levity, and trying to convince myself that the vernal breeze was a bit vulgar too, and that I was enjoying myself hugely.

I had not yet taken a good look at Vanya; I always needed a little time to get acclimated to her presence before looking at her. Now I saw she was wearing a black silk skirt and a white pullover with a low V neck, and that her hairdo was especially sleek. She went on looking through her lorgnette at the open book—a pogromystic novelette by a Russian lady in Belgrade or Harbin. How high we were above the street, right up in the gentle, rumpled sky . . . The vacuum cleaner inside stopped its buzzing. "Uncle Pasha is dead," she said, lifting her head. "Yes, we got a telegram this morning."

What did I care if the existence of that jovial, half-witted old man had come to an end? But at the thought that, along with him, had died the happiest, the shortest-lived image of Smurov, the image of Smurov the bridegroom, I felt that I could not restrain any more the agitation that had long been welling within me. I do not know how it started—there must have been some preparatory motions—but I remember finding myself perching on the wide wicker arm of Vanya's chair, and already clutching her wrist—that long-dreamt-of, forbidden contact. She blushed violently, and her eyes suddenly began to shine with tears—how clearly I saw her dark lower eyelid fill with glistening moisture. At the same time she kept smiling—as though with unexpected generosity she wished to bestow on me all the various expressions of her beauty. "He was such an amusing old man," she said to explain the radiance on her lips, but I interrupted her:

"I can't go on like this, I can't stand it any longer," I mumbled, now snatching her wrist, which would immediately grow tense, now turning an obedient leaf in the book on her lap, "I have to tell you . . . It doesn't make any difference now—I am leaving and shall never see you again. I have to tell you. After all, you don't know me . . . But actually I wear a mask—I am always hidden behind a mask . . ."

"Come, come," said Vanya, "I know you very well indeed, and I see everything, and understand everything. You are a good, intelligent person. Wait a moment, I'll take my handkerchief. You're sitting on it. No, it fell down. Thank you. Please let go of my hand—you mustn't touch me like that. Please, don't."

She was smiling anew, assiduously and comically raising her eyebrows, as if inviting me to smile too, but I had lost all control of myself, and some impossible hope was fluttering near me; I went on talking and gesticulating so wildly that the wicker chair arm creaked under me, and there were moments when the parting in Vanya's hair was right under my lips, whereupon she would carefully move her head away.

"More than life itself," I was saying rapidly, "more than life itself, and already for a long time, since the very first moment. And you are the first person that has ever told me that I am good . . ."

"Please don't," pleaded Vanya. "You are only hurting yourself, and me. Look, why don't you let me tell you how Roman Bogdanovich made a declaration of love to me. It was hilarious . . ."

"Don't you dare," I cried. "Who cares about that clown? I know, I know you would be happy with me. And, if there is anything about me that you don't like, I'll change—in any way you wish, I'll change."

"I like everything about you," said Vanya, "even your poetic imagination. Even your propensity to exaggerate at times. But above all I like your kindness—for you are very kind, and love everyone very much, and then you're always so absurd and charming. All the same, though, please stop grabbing my hand, or I shall simply get up and leave."

"So there is hope after all?" I asked.

"Absolutely none," said Vanya. "And you know it perfectly well yourself. And besides, he should be here any minute now."

"You cannot love him," I shouted. "You are deceiving yourself. He is not worthy of you. I could tell you some awful things about him."

"That will be enough," said Vanya and made as if to get up. But at this point, wishing to arrest her movement, I involuntarily and uncomfortably embraced her, and at the warm, woolly, transparent feel of her pullover a turbid, excruciating delight began to bubble within me; I was ready for anything, even for the most revolting torture, but I had to kiss her at least once.

"Why are you struggling?" I babbled. "What

can it cost you? For you it's only a little act of charity—for me, it's everything."

I believe I might have consummated a shiver of oneirotic rapture had I been able to hold her a few seconds longer; but she managed to free herself and stand up. She moved away to the balcony railing, clearing her throat and narrowing her eyes at me, and somewhere in the sky there rose a long harp-like vibration—the final note. I had nothing more to lose. I blurted out everything, I shouted that Mukhin did not and could not love her, in a torrent of triteness I depicted the certainty of our happiness if she married me, and, finally, feeling that I was about to break into tears, threw down her book, which somehow I happened to be holding, and turned to go, forever leaving Vanya on her balcony, with the wind, with the hazy spring sky, and with the mysterious bass sound of an invisible airplane.

In the parlor, not far from the door, Mukhin sat smoking. He followed me with his eyes and said calmly, "I never thought you were such a scoundrel." I saluted him with a curt nod of the head and left.

I descended to my room, took my hat, and hurried out into the street. Upon entering the first flower shop I saw, I began tapping my heel and whistling, as there was no one in sight. The enchantingly fresh aroma of flowers all around me stimulated my voluptuous impatience. The street continued in the side mirror adjoining the display window, but this was but an illusionary continuation: a car that had passed from left to right would vanish abruptly, even though the street awaited it imperturbably; another car, which had been approaching from the opposite direction, would vanish as well—one of them had been only a reflection. Finally the salesgirl appeared. I selected a big bouquet of lilies of the valley; cold gems dripped from their resilient bells, and the salesgirl's fourth finger was bandaged—must have pricked herself. She went behind the counter and for a long time fussed and rustled with a lot of nasty paper. The tightly bound stems formed a thick, rigid sausage; never had I imagined that lilies of the valley could be so heavy. As I pushed the door, I noticed the reflection in the side mirror: a young man in a derby carrying a bouquet, hurried toward me. That reflection and I merged into one. I walked out into the street.

I walked in extreme haste, with mincing steps, surrounded by a cloudlet of floral moisture, trying not to think about anything, trying to believe in the marvelous healing power of the particular place toward which I hurried. Going there was the only way to avert disaster: life, hot and burdensome, full of the familiar torment, was about to bear down on me again and rudely disprove that I was a ghost. It is frightening when real life suddenly turns out to be a dream, but how much more frightening when that which one had thought a dream—fluid and irresponsible—suddenly starts to congeal into reality! I had to put a stop to this, and I knew how to do it.

Upon reaching my destination, I began to press the button of the bell, without pausing to catch my breath; I rang as if quenching an unbearable thirst—lengthily, greedily, in utter self-oblivion. "All right, all right, all right," she grumbled, opening the door. I dashed across the threshold and thrust the bouquet into her hands.

"Oh, how beautiful!" she said, and, a little bewildered, fixed me with her old, pale-blue eyes.

"Don't thank me," I shouted, impetuously raising my hand, "but do me one favor: allow me to have a look at my old room. I implore you."

"The room?" said the old lady. "I'm sorry, but unfortunately it is not free. But how beautiful, how nice of you——"

"You didn't quite understand me," I said, quivering with impatience. "I only want to have a look. That's all. Nothing more. For the flowers I brought you. Please. I'm sure the roomer has gone to work . . ."

Deftly slipping past her, I ran along the corridor, and she came after me. "Oh dear, the room is rented," she kept repeating. "Dr. Galgen has no intention of leaving. I can't let you have it."

I yanked the door open. The furniture was somewhat differently distributed; a new pitcher stood on the washstand; and, on the wall behind it I found the hole, carefully plastered over—yes, the moment I found it I felt reassured. With my hand pressed to my heart I gazed at the secret mark of my bullet: it was my proof that I had really died; the world immediately regained its reassuring insignificance—I was strong once again, nothing could hurt me. With one sweep of my fancy I was ready to evoke the most fearsome shade from my former existence.

With a dignified bow to the old woman I left this room where, once upon a time, a man had bent over double as he released the fatal spring. In passing through the front hall, I noticed my flowers lying on the table and, feigning absent-mindedness, scooped them up, telling myself that the stupid old woman little deserved such an expensive gift. In fact, I could send it to Vanya, with a note both sad and humorous. The moist freshness of the flowers felt good; the thin paper had yielded here and there, and, squeezing with my fingers the cool green body of the stems, I recalled the gurgling and dripping that had accompanied me into nothingness. I walked leisurely along the very edge of the sidewalk and, half-closing my eyes, imagined that I was moving along the rim of a precipice, when a voice suddenly hailed me from behind.

"Gospodin Smurov," it said in a loud but hesitant tone. I turned at the sound of my name, involuntarily stepping off the sidewalk with one foot. It was Kashmarin, Matilda's husband, and he was pulling off a yellow glove, in a terrific hurry to proffer me his hand. He was without the famous cane, and had changed somehow—perhaps he had put on weight. There was an embarrassed expression on his face, and his large, lusterless teeth were simultaneously gritting at the rebellious glove and grinning at me. At last his hand, with out-spread fingers, fairly gushed toward me. I felt an odd weakness; I was deeply touched; my eyes even began to smart.

"Smurov," he said, "you can't imagine how glad I am to have run into you. I've been searching for you frantically but nobody knew your address."

Here it dawned upon me that I was listening much too politely to this apparition from my former life, and, deciding to take him down a peg or two, I said, "I have nothing to discuss with you. You should be grateful I did not take you to court."

"Look, Smurov," he said plaintively, "I'm trying to apologize for my vile temper. I couldn't live at peace with myself after our—uh—heated discussion. I felt horrible about it. Allow me to confess something to you, as one gentleman to another. You see, I learned after-wards that you were neither the first nor the last, and I divorced her—yes, divorced her."

"There can be no question of you and me discussing anything," I said, and took a sniff of my fat, cold bouquet.

"Oh, don't be so spiteful!" exclaimed Kash-marin. "Come on, hit me, give me a good punch, and then we'll make up. You don't want to? There, you're smiling—that's a good sign. No, don't hide behind those flowers—I can see you're smiling. So, now we can talk like friends. Allow me to ask how much money you are making."

I pouted awhile longer, and then answered him. All along I had to restrain a desire to say something nice, something to show how touched I was.

"Well, then, look," said Kashmarin. "I'll get you a job that pays three times as much. Come and see me tomorrow morning at the Hotel Monopole. I'll introduce you to a useful person. The job is a snap, and trips to the Riviera and to Italy are not to be ruled out. Automobile business. You'll stop by, then?"

He had, as they say, hit the bull's-eye. I had long been fed up with Weinstock and his books. I started sniffing at the cold flowers again, hiding in them my joy and my gratitude.

"I'll think it over," I said, and sneezed.

"God bless you!" exclaimed Kashmarin. "Don't forget then—tomorrow. I'm so glad, so very glad I ran into you."

We parted. I ambled on slowly, my nose buried in the bouquet.

Kashmarin had borne away yet another

image of Smurov. Does it make any difference which? For I do not exist: there exist but the thousands of mirrors that reflect me. With every acquaintance I make, the population of phantoms resembling me increases. Somewhere they live, somewhere they multiply. I alone do not exist. Smurov, however, will live on for a long time. The two boys, those pupils of mine, will grow old, and some image or other of me will live within them like a tenacious parasite. And then will come the day when the last person who remembers me will die. A fetus in reverse, my image, too, will dwindle and die within that last witness of the crime I committed by the mere fact of living. Perhaps a chance story about me, a simple anecdote in which I figure, will pass on from him to his son or grandson, and so my name and my ghost will appear fleetingly here and there for some time still. Then will come the end.

And yet I am happy. Yes, happy. I swear, I swear I am happy. I have realized that the only happiness in this world is to observe, to spy, to watch, to scrutinize oneself and others, to be nothing but a big, slightly vitreous, somewhat bloodshot, unblinking eye. I swear that this is happiness. What does it matter that I am a bit cheap, a bit foul, and that no one appreciates all the remarkable things about me—my fantasy, my erudition, my literary gift . . . I am happy that I can gaze at myself, for any man is absorbing—yes, really absorbing! The world, try as it may, cannot insult me. I am invulnerable. And what do I care if she marries another? Every other night I dream of her dresses and things on an endless clothesline of bliss, in a ceaseless wind of possession, and her husband shall never learn what I do to the silks and fleece of the dancing witch. This is love's supreme accomplishment. I am happy—yes, happy! What more can I do to prove it, how to proclaim that I am happy? Oh, to shout it so that all of you believe me at last, you cruel, smug people . . .

About the Author

Vladimir Nabokov was born in St. Petersburg on April 23, 1899. His family fled to the Crimea in 1917, during the Bolshevik Revolution, then went into exile in Europe. Nabokov studied at Trinity College, Cambridge, earning a degree in French and Russian literature in 1922, and lived in Berlin and Paris for the next two decades, writing prolifically, mainly in Russian, under the pseudonym Sirin. In 1940 he moved to the United States, where he pursued a brilliant literary career (as a poet, novelist, memoirist, critic, and translator) while teaching Russian, creative writing, and literature at Stanford, Wellesley, Cornell, and Harvard. The monumental success of his novel *Lolita* (1955) enabled him to give up teaching and devote himself fully to his writing. In 1961 he moved to Montreux, Switzerland, where he died in 1977. Recognized as one of the master prose stylists of the century in both Russian and English, he translated a number of his original English works—including *Lolita*—into Russian, and collaborated on English translations of his original Russian works.

ALSO BY VLADIMIR NABOKOV

ADA, OR ARDOR

Ada, or Ardor tells a love story troubled by incest. But more: it is also at once a fairy tale, an epic, and a philosophical treatise on the nature of time, a parody of the history of the novel, and an erotic catalogue.

Fiction/Literature/978-0-679-72522-0

BEND SINISTER

Bend Sinister is a haunting and compelling narrative about a civilized man caught in the tyranny of a police state. Professor Adam Krug, the country's foremost philosopher, offers the only hope of resistance to Paduk, dictator and leader of the Party of the Average Man.

Fiction/Literature/978-0-679-72727-9

THE ENCHANTER

The Enchanter is the Ur-*Lolita*, the precursor to Nabokov's classic novel. It tells the story of an outwardly respectable man and his fatal obsession with certain pubescent girls, whose coltish grace and subconscious coquetry reveal, to his mind, a bud on the verge of bloom.

Fiction/Literature/978-0-679-72886-3

THE GIFT

The Gift is an ode to Russian literature, evoking the works of Pushkin, Gogol, and others in the course of its narrative: the story of Fyodor Godunov-Cherdyntsev, an impoverished émigré poet living in Berlin, who dreams of the book he will someday write.

Fiction/Literature/978-0-679-72725-5

GLORY

Glory is the wryly ironic story of Martin Edelweiss, a young Russian émigré of no account, who is in love with a girl who refuses to marry him. Hoping to impress his love, he embarks on a "perilous, daredevil project"—to illegally reenter the Soviet Union.

Fiction/Literature/978-0-679-72724-8

INVITATION TO A BEHEADING

In a dream country, the young man Cincinnatus C. is condemned to death by beheading for "gnostical turpitude," an imaginary crime that defies definition. Cincinnatus spends his last days in an absurd jail, where he is visited by chimerical jailers, an executioner who masquerades as a fellow prisoner, and by his in-laws.

Fiction/Literature/978-0-679-72531-2

KING, QUEEN, KNAVE

Dreyer, a wealthy and boisterous proprietor of a men's clothing store is ruddy, self-satisfied, and masculine, but he is repugnant to his exquisite but cold middle-class wife, Martha. Attracted to his money but repelled by his oblivious passion, she longs for their nephew instead.

Fiction/Literature/978-0-679-72340-0

LAUGHTER IN THE DARK

Albinus, a respectable, middle-aged man and aspiring filmmaker, abandons his wife for a lover half his age: Margot, who wants to become a movie star herself. When Albinus introduces her to Rex, an American movie producer, disaster ensues.

Fiction/Literature/978-0-679-72450-6

LOLITA

Awe and exhilaration—along with heartbreak and mordant wit—abound in *Lolita*, Nabokov's most famous and controversial novel, which tells the story of the aging Humbert Humbert's obsessive, devouring, and doomed passion for the nymphet Dolores Haze.

Fiction/Literature/978-0-679-72316-5

THE ANNOTATED LOLITA
Edited by Alfred Appel, Jr.

The Annotated Lolita is the definitive annotated text of the modern classic. It assiduously glosses *Lolita*'s extravagant wordplay and its frequent literary allusions, parodies, and cross references.

Fiction/Literature/978-0-679-72729-3

LOOK AT THE HARLEQUINS!

This novel is the autobiography of the eminent Russian-American author Vadim Vadimovich N. (b. 1899). Focusing on the central figures of his life—his four wives, his books, and his muse, Dementia—the book leads us to suspect that the fictions Vadim has created have crossed the line between his life's work and his life itself.

Fiction/Literature/978-0-679-72728-6

MARY

In a Berlin rooming house filled with an assortment of seriocomic Russian émigrés, Lev Ganin, once a vigorous young officer, relives his idyllic first love affair with Mary in pre-revolutionary Russia. In stark contrast to his memories is the unappealing boarder living in the room next to his, who, he later discovers, is Mary's husband, separated from her by the Revolution but expecting her arrival.

Fiction/Literature/978-0-679-72620-3

PALE FIRE

In *Pale Fire*, Nabokov offers a cornucopia of deceptive pleasures: a 999-line poem by the reclusive genius John Shade; an adoring foreword and commentary by Shade's self-styled Boswell, Dr. Charles Kinbote; a darkly comic novel of suspense, literary idolatry and one-upmanship, and political intrigue.

Fiction/Literature/978-0-679-72342-4

PNIN

A professor of Russian at an American college, Pnin takes the wrong train to deliver a lecture in a language he cannot master. Although he is the focal point of subtle academic conspiracies he cannot begin to comprehend, he stages the faculty party to end all faculty parties.

Fiction/Literature/978-0-679-72341-7

TRANSPARENT THINGS

"*Transparent Things* revolves around the four visits of the hero—sullen, gawky Hugh Person—to Switzerland. . . . As a young publisher, Hugh is sent to interview R., falls in love with Armande on the way, wrests her, after multiple humiliations, from a grinning Scandinavian and returns to New York with his bride. . . . Eight years later—following a murder, a period of madness and a brief imprisonment—Hugh makes a lone sentimental journey to wheedle out his past" (Martin Amis).

Fiction/Literature/978-0-679-72541-1

VINTAGE INTERNATIONAL
Available from your local bookstore, or visit

Printed in the United States
by Baker & Taylor Publisher Services